KELLY'S FULL HOUSE

Paddy Kelly

KELLY'S FULL HOUSE

FICTION4ALL

INTRODUCTION

They say everything comes in threes. Here's three rib tickling tales featuring three characters in three very different time periods and situations.

An octogenarian paediatrician with nothing left to lose, a young NYC reporter who has one last chance to save the beleaguered, glossy magazine she works for and a puzzled librarian who accidently discovers a mysterious document signed by George Washington himself on the date of the outbreak of American Revolution.

Kelly's Full House is a great short story collection that will lift your spirits and help get you through your day by dealing with some of the most taboo subjects – The Press, death and politics.

127 Alden Road

For

The most important two little pilgrims in my life:

Katherine Mary
&
Erin Elizabeth

American History

†

Monday Morning, 26th of June
Provincetown, Massachusetts

"MY DADDY ALWAYS said that if'n it was a man's intent to lead a full life he ought to get out and about. He didn't mean just past the chicken coup, over old man Johnson's brook out into the woods or even out beyond the south forty. He meant outta Arkansas all together.

So when Mary Jane Kapeckni down to the Tic Toc Diner told me her sister-in-law's brother's cousin's sister said there was work up north and they was looking for experienced school janitorial staff, I sent my particulars out straight away and a week later I was on a Greyhound north.

Time sure flies and I can't hardly believe how fast the last eleven years has flew, but they done flown and that there in a nut shell is how I, Eugene Amos Corn, came to be in Provincetown, Massachusetts. P-town to the natives.

P-town is as peaceful a place I guess you're gonna find in these parts. Small, quiet, and real friendly. Takes some getting' used to though, especially the way everybody here talks with a real funny accent like. Not with proper grammatizin' like back down in Hogwalla County. But real friendly folks just the same.

Course some'a the visitors can get a little too friendly if ya know what I mean. 'Specially in the summertime when we get invaded by all the city slickers from Boston and some'a their men folk keep dressin' up like women an all.

Being only 115 miles outta' the state capital west on

State Route number six, it's real rural like but, there's some interesting things to be found.

Take that tall, stone tower over there, the highest point in Barnstable County! Fact! Folks call that the Pilgrim Mon-u-ment.

Most folks, me included thanks to Mrs. Schmedly back in fourth grade history, grew up under the impression that when them there English people first come over to this country they landed at Plymouth Rock. Turns out they actually landed right here in P-town first! Fact!

Why anyone would name a rock after a big, expensive car is a mystery to me, but, these Yankees never was known for the logical way they do stuff. But it's a certifiable fact. They was here first.

Was also right here they drew up this thing called the Mayflower Compact, a bunch'a rules and stuff they swore to live by. Kind'a like a contract I guess.

Anyway, I digress. I'm supposed to be talking to ya'll about the big fuss kicked up about that old building over at 127 Alden Road. That's that building right over there, the little black timber frame covered in clapboards. Small but pretty. That's Reverend Bingham's Ninth Day Adventist Church. Since the Eighth Day Adventist Church closed up and moved out to Cambridge folks here just call it 127 Alden or the church.

Alaster Kindred, an old black fella from back home come up here one time to visit his daughter, seen Bingham's church and scratched his head. I asked him what was the matter.

'Most little wooden churches down in our neck of the woods,' he said, '. . . is painted white and has black folks inside! First time I ever seen a black church with white folks on the inside!' We had a good laugh but old Alester never did have time to learn about 127.

I remember all the hub bub like it was just last year ..."

The Discovery
†

It was in July of 2017 and Abigail Helmsworth, town librarian, archivist and charter member of the Ladies of New England Social Organization for Massachusetts History, was doing some spring cleaning in her office in back of the Herman Melville Memorial Library over on Commercial Street.

The fact that the social organization membership was exclusively composed of widowed or divorced women over sixty accounted for the fact that they were generally referred to by the town's folk as the LONESOME's. They didn't take too kindly to that name.

The walls of Abigail's office were profusely adorned with a plethora of certificates, awards and photographs of important looking people shaking hands with other not as important looking people as they handed over awards of various shapes and descriptions.

It was just after nine in the morning and Abagail was stuck into a her cleaning frenzy when she went looking for Bob the Handyman who was nowhere to be found now that Jimmy Kelly's Pub over on Cornwell Street was open and you could get a beer and a whiskey with your bowl of chowder if you ate in the back room so's the Sheriff couldn't see ya.

That being the case Abagail, no stranger to a fish supper herself if you catch my drift, decided on wrestling back the old steel filing cabinet on her own to get in and clean behind it.

A half dozen grunts, several expletives directed at Bob the Handyman and a few drops of sweat later the big steel cabinet was cocked just enough away from the wall that she could get behind it.

She glanced down and sittin' in the dust and debris Abagail spied a funny looking folder leaning against the Canadian maple base board and the white oak judge's paneling which surrounded the room.

Funny looking because she hadn't seen that particular style of envelope since she was a little girl way back in . . . back when . . . a long time ago. After dusting off the sturdy, chocolate brown, accordion folder and unwinding the brown cord from the grommets holding it closed she was amazed to find only two sheets of paper inside. A letter with some notes scribbled on the back of it and a deed of some sort. A very old deed on what Abagail guessed was two or three hundred year old parchment.

She knew it to be a deed mainly because the word 'DEED' was stamped across the top of the document.

With the due diligence of a town archivist Abigail took the papers over to her desk, switched on the green glass shaded desk lamp and read.

She decided to attack the letter first.

Abagail didn't get much out of it other than it was dated December sixth, 1941, because it contained a short two or three sentence message to a lawyer from another lawyer all written in lawyerese.

She set it aside and reached for her one inch thick magnifying glass mounted on its flexible swing arm, donned her Spec-Saver glasses and perused the document.

Abagail read, took a breath, sat back and it was nearly a full minute before she breathed again. Leaning forward she reread the bottom of the document for the third time.

Waddling at the top speed of one and a half miles per hour, Abagail Helmsworth burst from her office, through the front door and out onto Commercial Street with all the grace of a wounded baby hippo just been darted by a well-meaning zoologist on the Serengeti.

Perfectly penned across the bottom of the deed, dated this 'Thrtyith Day of June, In This The Year of Lord 1775', was the signature of George Washington, General of the Continental Army and first president of the United States.

†

The next day this revelation of The Revolution was revealed at a special ad hoc meeting of the ladies club wherein the big news was released.

That morning at ten sharp in the little lecture room of the library a dozen women shuffled in and took their seats. An overhead projector stood next to the podium and the emergency meeting of the LONESOME's began.

Mrs. Hannah Higgins, five time President and charter member of the LONESOME's, took to the podium and called what was, by some accounts, the fourteenth emergency meeting that year to order.

An upright, forthright and what some still referred to as a 'proper lady', Higgins was not only the richest individual of all the 2,723 residents of P-town, she was the one of the most well informed in regards to everyone else's business. But at least she came by her money honestly. She married into it.

Her former, now deceased, husband was a prominent doctor, a well-known and successful speech therapist who it is rumored suffered a massive coronary one day when he accidently heard Sylvester Stallone speak in a film while Snoop Dogg music was playing in the background.

With a gentle, lady-like tap of the gavel Hannah called the meeting to order and with little introduction but with great reluctance invited Abagail to speak.

As was most things in P-town it was common knowledge that Higgins carried a grudge against Abagail ever since the librarian had the audacity, however politely, to suggest at the AGM a few years back, that perhaps the membership, all twelve of them, should consider rotating the society's presidency.

It was with no small amount of trepidation that Mrs. Higgins attended the meeting, harboring strong feelings that the society was yet again taking away valuable meeting time when they could be planting fresh azalea bushes along the footpath to the town hall before the deadline for the county Tidy Towns Award judges panel came through in August.

For her part Abigail paid no mind to Higgins's begrudgery putting it down to age, her solitary lifestyle and perhaps lowered lithium levels in her blood serum.

The newly discovered document now safely sealed in glass and tucked under her arm, it was with barely contained excitement that Abagail took the stage.

"Ladies, yesterday while doing my Spring cleaning-"

"IT'S JULY ALREADY! WHO DOES SPRING CLEANING IN JULY?!" The fanged voice of Higgins cried out from the back of the room.

"Those of us who have a job and not livin' off the profits of our husbands!" Abagail fired back. Amidst the uncomfortable silence there were a few giggles and Abagail soldiered on.

"Yesterday while doing my spring cleaning . . ." Abagail paused and glanced to the back. Higgins crossed her arms and legs and let out a muffled 'harumpf'.

"Yesterday while doing my spring cleaning I found something I think will not only help to re-write U.S. history but put P-town back on the map and most importantly boost the prestige of the Ladies of New England Society as well as revitalize the respect this organization had enjoyed in the years past!"

Anticipation mounted.

"Can someone in the back of the room please turn off the lights?" All eyes swung around to look at the back of the room where, tucked in the corner Higgins sat by herself, huddled on her wooden folding chair, quietly scowling. Reluctantly she complied and the compact lecture hall went dark.

The screen behind the podium flashed on and, taking up the remote plunger, Abagail clicked to the first slide.

"This appears to be some kind of letter I found with the document, the only two things in the folder." At the word 'document' mumbling began to simmer to the surface.

In the back Higgins turned away from the screen but snuck one eyeball slightly to the left to sneak a peek.

"I sent a photo of it over to Cohen, Cohen & Cohen law offices to help us with the translation."

Murmurs of agreement dusted over the group.

"But this!" She changed slides. "This is 'the document'! The most important document, I believe to be found in these parts since the *Mayflower Compact*!"

At the utterance of '*The Mayflower Compact*', all bowed their heads in silence. Even Higgins.

"It's a deed. A deed signed and approved by none other than . . ." Again she changed slides and a close up of the signatory line of the deed came up. ". . . our very first president, George Washington!"

Shutting down the projector she held aloft the carefully, glass encased parchment deed for all to view. Of her own accord Higgins flicked back on the lights and, as did all the others, scurried to the front of the room to get a closer look.

"This deed, dated June thirtieth, 1775 appears to be the original deed to Reverend Bingham's church at 127 Alden Road!" Abagail gleefully informed.

It was amidst a fever pitch of excitement not seen since May of 1938 when FDR's motorcade stopped at Frank Comming's Feed & Grain so the President could take a pee, that the women gathered as if Elvis Presley himself were handing out autographs. They scurried to circle around and get a glimpse of the glass ensconced parchment, the signature and the particulars contained there-in.

For her part, and much to her credit, Higgins made her way up to the crowd where the gaggle of giggly ladies parted and took hold of the document.

After an acceptable silence she spoke.

"Abagail you have done very well. Congratulations."

Good karma once again reigned.

"However-"

Suddenly there was a disturbance in The Force.

"We must decide exactly what to do with this possibly

valuable, potentially authentic artifact!"

"Potentially authentic?! What do you mean? Exactly?" Abagail demanded.

"There are laws in the Commonwealth of Massachusetts. One cannot just go around finding pieces of paper stamped 'two hundred year old document' and hang them on the wall as if they were a certificate of participation in a spelling bee!" Higgins authoritatively informed.

"What kind of laws?!" Someone demanded.

"This has to be authenticated! For all we know some prankster might have printed this out on his laptop! He might have made it up at home using Picture Shop or something!"

"It's Photoshop!" Someone else corrected.

"Whatever the kids are calling it-" Hannah continued but Mrs. O'Keefe, operator of the local greens grocer, interrupted.

"Mrs. Higgins, I move, and I think most of the girls here will agree, that we should have a town gala and show off this fantastic discovery of Abagail's." Polite applause and head shaking was taken as a mandate. "Maybe even get some local press so people can know about this."

"Why not set it for next Tuesday?!" One of the

women suggested.

"On the Fourth! That's a great idea!" O'Keefe seconded.

"LADIES, ladies, ladies! Let's not lose the run of ourselves!" Higgins intended to go down swinging.

"What now Mrs. Higgins?!"

"Abagail Helmsworth you of all people should know that in the 18th Century it was illegal to hold, demand or negotiate a deed for church property!"

"EXACTLY!" Abagail shouted. Higgins was taken aback, shocked by Abagail's agreement. "You're absolutely correct Hannah! It was against commonwealth laws to profit by or charge clergy or church officials for property used for worship or prayer meetings!" Higgins was left speechless by Helmsworth's concession. "That's exactly why the church had to be something else! It had to be used for another purpose! If we can find out what it was, we can add another chapter to the fascinating story that is Provincetown!" More golf claps erupted.

"Perhaps it was mixed up with someone else's property?" O'Keefe suggested.

"Or it could have been an inn of some sort."

"Right then! I move we plan the gala for the Fourth which gives us a week to get authentication from Boston and prepare a story for the P-town Gazette!"

"Hold on!" It was Higgins again. "We cannot proceed with what I am relatively certain will ultimately turn out to be nothing more than a wild goose chase!"

"What are you talking about Hannah?"

"Simply that state confirmation may not be enough. We may have to submit this piece of paper, clearly of unknown origin, to a federally appointed agency."

"Oh Hannah, give over will you for cryin' out loud!" It was Mel Mead newly arrived from San Antonio, Texas back in the 1970's. "Why can't you give it a rest! We got something here to be proud of and all you wanna

19

do is piss all over it you bitter old bat!"

Wide spread giggling seemed to have extinguished Higgins' fire, at least for the moment.

Following a further one hour discussion it was decided that the LONESOMES would host a grand town gala which would be to celebrate the 240th anniversary of the founding of what could have been a farm house, a road side inn, another church or some other building of unknown function on what was now 127 Alden Road, on the main pyke to Boston.

In the end the women voted on taking a vote, to make it official, which they did and the vote was passed unanimously. Almost.

There was one abstention.

The Church

†

The Right Reverend Cecil T. Bingham, like all of the town elders, was born right there in P-town. A practical man in most matters however there were only three areas in which, as far as he was concerned, there was no room for discussion or compromise. God and his flying insect collection.

Until science could definitively show that man had descended from the monkeys, an obvious lie as no man the good reverend had ever met had a tail, there was nothing to contradict the word of The Almighty. That being the case all else fell to logic for which any questions, comments or snide remarks could quite simply be explained by the Good Book, both volumes of which Cecil had practically memorized. And he had no hesitation to explain in excruciating detail exactly where the Jews got it wrong in the first edition. He liked the sequel much better.

Now Cecil had a wife, Georgina.

Georgina came from a good New England family and was as faithful a wife as a man could ask for, content in assuming the domestic duties of a traditional spouse.

She accompanied the reverend to service each Sunday morning at 10:00 sharp then, an hour later, stood by the back door of the church to shake hands and thank the few parishioners who still showed up for worship.

Together Cecil and Georgina made a lovely couple. However, the otherwise happy betrothed was cursed by God who in his infinite wisdom had denied the pious pair the ability to bear children.

For the first five years of their marriage Georgina and Cecil enthusiastically engaged the beast with two backs four to five times a week and thrust themselves into the effort which resulted in a strained lumbar, two extremely exhausted people and $1,125 in chiropractor bills.

All with no results.

Religious faith undeterred, the two prayed and dreamt, dreamt and prayed and prayed some more.

Finally it was decided upon to resort to government assistance.

For two long years applications followed forms, long forms and short forms, preceded by documents interspersed with interviews until, one sunny day, the post man brought the good news and the Binghams were able to thank the Almighty that they were born into a country with relatively liberal adoption laws.

And so it came to pass that the State Board of Adoption of the great Commonwealth of Massachusetts begat Catherine to the Binghams, an infant whose own parents had tragically been taken in a road accident when she was only a few months old.

A happy family had been born.

Meanwhile, unaware of the archeological anomaly being debated that morning over in the library concerning the old timber frame and clapboard building at 127 Alden Road, now Pastor Bingham's Ninth Day Adventist church, the Reverend happily putzed around the place accompanied by his lovely daughter Catherine, now a mature-for-her-age, budding 18 year old, helping out with collecting the hymnals from yesterday's service.

It was a nervous Catherine who attempted to muster the courage to broach a subject with her father she had been waiting more than a month to discuss. That subject being the handsome Jimmy O'Keefe son of the local greens grocers and home for the summer from college.

Now, the only thing that rivaled Cecil T.'s denial of the facts put forth by the entire scientific community, biologically speaking visa vie the 'E' word, E for evolution, was the reality of the romantic infatuation of his progeny, of which there was only the one. This romantic infatuation felt by his daughter was a very, very sore spot at the present stage of the reverend's and Catherine's familial relationship. But being a brave young woman she decided to charge the enemy.

"Dad?" Catherine quietly called across the aisle as she purposely took her time collecting up the hymnals.

"Yes Sweetheart?"

"Everybody's pretty excited about the big Fourth of July celebration coming up, especially the dance that night. We never had one like this. I hear they're bringing a band all the way in from New Jersey!"

"Seems a bit daft to me. We got plenty'a bands right here on the Cape. Besides, the Fourth's the time folks should be praying to God in thanks for this beautiful land kept free by the blood and sweat of the brave soldiers and sailors who fought for it."

"Uh huh." Catherine chose her next words carefully. "Father, I hear Jimmy O'Keefe is home from college in Boston." Cecil dropped a hymnal and an audible grunt echoed from nave to alter.

"He's not in school in Boston. He's only in Worcester!"

"That's only because B.C. didn't have an opening on their rugby team this year. But next year-"

"Rugby! An animal's game! God had intended man to bang heads He'd'a given us horns!"

"Next year-"

"Next year we might all be dead and in heaven! Well, most of us anyway. Probably not those damned Republicans! And what kind of profession is he chasing after that he's got time to play at boy's games?"

"You know full well! I told you a half dozen times what he's studying!"

"Politics no doubt. Probably turn out to be a socialist or communist! Or worse yet a Republican!"

"Republicans, Democrats what's the difference?!

They're all politicians. One lies and the others all swear to it!"

"CATHERINE! That's no way to speak about the freest country in the world, young lady!"

"Yeah free for everyone except the last girl in senior year of high school without a boyfriend! You know how embarrassing it is to have to make excuses for telling people you're not going to the Fourth of July dance?!"

Cecil stopped and looked over at his daughter.

"Catherine . . ." She ignored him. He persisted. "Has he asked you yet?"

"No, how could he?! Everyone in the town knows how you feel about his family!" Cecil laid his hymnals down and crossed the aisle over to her.

"Sweetheart, I don't hate his family! It's just that . . .just that-"

"Just that they don't belong to Pastor Bingham's Ninth Day Adventist church! Ohhh! Heresy!"

"They don't belong to any church! Those O'Keefe's have even been seen working on Sunday. More than once mind you!"

"So?! People need groceries on Sunday same as any other day! People don't stop eating just because it's Sunday!"

"So how would it look if the pastor's daughter was seen around town keeping company with the son of a heathen?!"

"Just like the Democrats and Republicans. It's not what's best for the people it's only about my way not your way!"

"Catherine I just need you to see-"

"I see alright, I see essentially nothing's changed here since 1692! That's what I see!" Catherine angrily declared as she stomped down the aisle and out of the back door of the church.

Cecil's fell back into a seat as his heart sank lower than a democrat and republican trying to agree on passing a bill.

✝

Planning for the nation's birthday celebration was no small matter in P-town and folks took that day, and the day before that and the day after, very serious, especially on that weekend when the town's population was expected to swell from just under 3,000 to upwards of 60,000 or more.

Details for organizing such a suspicious occasion generally fell to Lester Hickam, President of the town council, so Abagail considered Lester's office the logical place to start her campaign for permission to initiate an official gala celebrating the document.

That afternoon, in his office, she methodically explained to Councilman Hickham her thoughts on approaching the matter and the potential moral, historical and especially financial benefits to the town and potentially to all of eastern Barnstable County.

After a rapid-fire, half hour pitch Lester asked a few questions and, satisfied with the answers, told Abagail that he would get behind her initiative but added that he thought it would be a good idea to run it by Jon Carver, P-town's mayor.

With the excitement of a little kid at bedtime on Christmas Eve Abigail scurried across the street, her satchel containing the document tucked tightly under her arm, to Carver's Hardware Store.

Jon Carver's office was situated in the back of *Carver's All American Hardware – Founded in 1701* originally as a trading post and later, as the town blossomed, a dedicated hardware store. It was the largest and most expansive commercial business in town.

General housewares, ironware and kitchenware were stocked. Everything from a thumbtack to a railway spike could be had at old man Carver's. Whether it was a

25

gasket for your kitchen faucet or a ten foot length of copper tubing you could find it at Craver's. If he didn't have it in stock he guaranteed to have it in from Boston in 48 hours.

It was here that Abagail now made her way down the creaky wooden floor of the long central aisle. Down around the power tool rack past the rotating bins of steel screws, under the multitude of hanging tools, implements and utensils which dangled from the ceiling to the back of the shop where Mayor Carver looked up and spied her through the small sliding, Plexiglas window beside his desk. He lowered his feet, dropped his Wall Street Journal and slid the window closed.

The feelings of consternation and dread which seized him were hidden by the phony smile painted across his face as their eyes met. A visit from a member of the LONESOME's never ended well. Like the time a year or so back when they petitioned Carver for permission to have a bake sale on Commercial Street with the proceeds going to the Mexican Orphans' Fund in Boston and half the town came down with dysentery. It was the last time Doris Huntsacker was allowed to sell burritos.

Jon Carver, five-time Mayor of P-town and sole owner of Carver's, had parlayed his family's business into a multi-million dollar corporation whose opulence and true worth was masked by the one shop tucked away in the small settlement of P-town.

Jon rose from desk and with extended hand moved to greet Abagail.

"Miss Helmsworth, what a pleasant surprise! How are you today?"

"Very, very excited Mr. Mayor!"

"Oh Abagail, how long have we known each other? There's no need for such formality! How can I help my favorite librarian today?"

"Well, Jon, yesterday while I was doing some spring cleaning, I was a little late this year, I found this!" She passed the document, pressed between two pieces of glass and now framed, across his desk. After a minute or so Carver commented.

"This is pretty amazing Abagail."

"I found it behind a cabinet and compared the signature to some photos I have in the archives and it matches perfectly! My idea is to launch a consecutive gala in conjunction with our annual celebrations during the day long festivities on the Fourth! You know to celebrate the discovery of the document."

"I see. Well, that's a fine idea Abagail, but has it been authenticated? Officially I mean. Look pretty damn silly if we go through all that and it turns out some kid made it up on his computer using Shop Photo."

"It's Photoshop Jon."

"Whatever. You get my point. I mean there's gonna be upwards of fifty, sixty thousand visitors here next weekend. You can imagine the headlines not to mention the repercussions if this thing isn't the genuine article!"

"But Jon, the celebration is this weekend! What can I do in four or five days? Official state certification could take months and cost thousands!" She pleaded.

With the reputation of P-town on the line Jon saw the dilemma. He became silent and sat back in his high-back leather chair expressing his consternation by declaring a loud, "Humm."

Being the highest official in town as well as the richest, he was anything but uncaring being certain to hit all the important charities throughout the ear and most of the minor ones as well.

After a long hard moment of thought he reached a conclusion.

"Tell ya what I can do Abagail. I have a friend at Harvard, the Dean of Humanities. I'll give him a ring and see if he can get ahold of somebody who can help us out. How's that?"

Flushed with more excitement then her wedding

night, or the night she lost her virginity, Abagail
waddled around the desk and hugged Jon Carver until he
turned a dark shade of light blue.

The Secret Rendezvous

†

The second oldest established business on Commercial Street was O'Keefe's Greens Grocer. The O'Keefe's may have been the richest family in Barnstable County but they never lost sight of the fact that it was the people who made them so.

To that end they were careful to keep their massive grocery store fully stocked at all times and always went that extra step to accommodate their clientele.

Special orders were treated with special care by Mrs. O'Keefe, personal requests were handled personally by Mr. O'Keefe and large orders were delivered anywhere in the county by big Jimmy O'Keefe in their extra-large truck.

Perhaps it was because O'Keefe's was nearly as old as Bingham's church that the good reverend was unable to assuage the animosity he felt for O'Keefe.

Some speculated that Bingham being of British heritage and O'Keefe being of Irish extraction is why sparks flew the few times they met. Or it could have just been that with Jim's father worshiping at the chapel of St. Pillow each Sunday instead of Pastor Bingham's church, things got off to a bad start twenty-five years ago when they first encountered each other. Whatever the cause relations between the two had been rocky ever since.

This animosity was the reason that Mrs. Bingham had to drive all the way over to Cape Cod to buy her consumables each week because, in her words, 'Cecil would have a cow' if he were to find out she had shopped at O'Keefe's in town, which she normally did by phoning her order in first then, being sure Cecil was deeply occupied elsewhere, would dash down the street and collect her foodstuffs at which time she would then

have to fib and tell him she drove over to the Cape Cod
A&P.

An extra $20 kept the Assistant Manager at the Cape
Cod A&P from asking questions when, every few
months, she would show up to purchase a bundle of
A&P shopping bags to replenish her secret stash.

So it was with great surprise that Mrs. Bingham
received the phone call she got from Mrs. O'Keefe
suggesting they meet that after noon just one day before
the big dinner.

It was over in a Cape Cod café the clandestine
rendezvous was carried out.

"Thank you for meeting me Mertyl."

"Don't mention it Maureen! Thank you for hiding
my A&P bags in your back store room all these years!"

"Men can be so silly sometimes!"

"Amen to that sister!"

"I hope you don't think me too forward but . . . I
want to talk to you about my Jimmy and your
Catherine."

"OH thank the Lord!" Mertyl declared as if her
biopsy results had just come back negative. Mrs.
O'Keefe, taken aback was greatly relieved. "I thought I
was the only one who saw it!"

"ONLY ONE WHO SAW IT?! The whole town's
been at it since Jimmy's returned from college! Until this
document thing popped up the two of them getting
together is all the LONESOME's have been gossiping
about day and night!"

"Gives them something to do I guess. It's virtually
every day after the chapel service that someone assaults
me!" Mertyl elaborated. "'Catherine met anyone yet?'
'Is your Catherine seeing anyone now days?' 'I've got
just the boy for your young Catherine!' Sometimes I
think the Hindus got it right with their arranged marriage
thing!"

"Funny you should mention arrangements, that's

30

exactly what I'd like to talk to you about."

"Okay, shoot! I'm all ears!"

"Well because those two blockheads-"

"You mean our two block heads?"

"Exactly! Because our two blockheads won't even talk to one another it's on us to make something happen. Do you agree?"

"One hundred and ten percent! What do you suggest?"

"Well, you got an invite to Abagail's dinner tomorrow night, no?"

"Yes I did, why?"

"I have a strong feeling that Jimmy is going to forget his cell phone tomorrow night when we leave the house to go to the dinner."

"But those young kids are never seen without their phones! You'd just as soon ask them to forget their-" Halted in midsentence by Maureen's Grinch-like smirk, Mertyl reciprocated.

✝

As the wives plotted, word of the document's discovery spread.

By mid-week, out in the big city, *The Boston Globe* had gotten wind of the find and organized plans to send a news crew out to cover the big day.

Due to Reuters and AP access, the news went national and because of You Tube, Face Book, Twitter and Instagram, MySpace the story went viral.

By that evening NYU wanted to send a team of archeologists to P-town, to dig for other possible riches.

When word reached them the LONESOME's weren't too keen and became worried sick that the deed might turn out to be fake. That is until informed there was a New York writer with a film producer attached who was interested in optioning the story rights.

The Dinner

†

It was Wednesday, June 28th which left less than a week to plan and coordinate the Gala of the Document with the annual Fourth of July celebration and the ladies' society quickly came to realize, as cantankerous as Hannah Higgins could be she was right that some sort of official state recognition would be needed to substantiate the document's authenticity.

The Mayor however, after having expressed the same sentiment as Higgins, did stay true to his word regarding help. He had contacted the Harvard Dean of Humanities at that fine old institution and called in a favor.

The chosen candidate, following approval of funds from the town council, would not only have to be qualified, certified and electrified about the project, but be steeped in U.S., New England and Cape history as well.

Founded in 1636 Harvard is the United States' oldest institution of higher learning as well as the oldest chartered corporation in the great Commonwealth of Massachusetts, one of the oldest in America and so the tentacles of her business connections reached far and wide.

One or two phone calls followed by three or four emails and the LONESOME's were in like Flynn as Jon Carver secured them an official from that grand old school. An official who was willing to examine the document and determine its authenticity. And so the frantic search initially anticipated was avoided.

Enter Professor Emiratis Jubile Q. Periwinkle, Ph.D., esteemed historian, renowned anthropologist and Fellow of the American College of International Historians, FAC-IT for short. More importantly he was known to be the direct descendent of the man who loaned Paul Revere his horse when Revere's own steed came down with a bad case of dyspepsia the eve of his famous midnight ride.

No one would ever have known the Redcoats were coming and there's no telling how many lives were saved by Old Paint that fateful night but it was certainly more than a few. Worse yet the Yankees would'a had had a picture of a queen on their money instead of a guy in a frilly white shirt and long powdered wig.

Fully aware of the magnitude of her time crunch situation Abagail strategically planned a dinner that Wednesday evening to greet the learned professor and boost the town's efforts.

That morning was spent at the library where, hastily shielded behind a sign declaring that due to an academic emergency the library would be closed that day, Abagail researched a suitable menu. The afternoon was spent food shopping.

By three o'clock she was back home, the oven blasting away at full tilt as she was laying out the best china, her finest silverware and was even motivated to rummage around her upstairs hope chest until she excavated the white linen table cloth aunt Hermione gave her for her wedding back in 19 . . . back during the . . . a long time ago.

The strategically scheduled seven course event was set for that evening at eight and, to further insure its success Abagail scheduled reinforcements.

Mayor Carver and Lester Hickam were invited as were the Reverend and Mrs. Bingham. The O'Keefe's received an invite and Abagail, knowing the Binghams would bring Catherine with, took pains to suggest they bring young Jimmy along.

Finally, by way of extending an olive branch, (more like a twig), Abagail even passed the word that Hannah Higgins was welcomed.

33

RSVP's were forthcoming with each invitee harboring their own personal reasons for accepting Abagail's kind solicitation.

There was no secret Abagail was hosting the dinner to boost efforts for the document to be authenticated but she also hoped to significantly increase the odds of a favorable reception by the rest of the town.

Professor Jubile Q. Periwinkle on the other hand RSVP'd to dinner and agreed to look over the document not out of the benevolence of his heart but partially because Jon Carver secretly offered him $500 from the city treasury. Surreptitiously Periwinkle was desperate to PR his latest book, "The Truth Behind Paul Revere's Midnight Ride", actually published five years ago and still not doing so well on the Amazon book charts. Between the secret fee and some book promo Jubile reasoned he could take a lot away from visiting P-town, not least of which was a free meal.

Mayor Jon Carver of course had a keen interest in making an appearance should any talk of public speeches, awards or dedications come up. Who better to make sure the dedication plaque, which there was surly to be one, had his name on it.

Pastor Cecil T. Bingham of course had a God-given duty to attend the dinner-meeting to make sure God would be included in all proceedings, agreements and arrangements. For surely it was only by the will of The Almighty that Bob the Handyman was down in Jimmy Kelly's Pub over on Cornwell Street that morning drinking beer and eating chowder which caused Abagail to have to move that filing cabinet by herself thus uncovering the said archeological treasure.

Motivated by the primary reason of making inroads into getting Jimmy O'Keefe to ask her to the Fourth of July dance, (preferably without her father knowing about it), Mary Bingham jumped at the chance when asked by her mother.

Councilman Bill Hickam had no problem announcing he would be there to add to the glory of P-town's history and fame. He forgot to mention he would also be there to help access Hannah Higgin's money.

Unfortunately Councilman Hickam was to be disappointed. Hannah Higgins, to Abagail's relief, took pains to announce that she would not be there to sabotage or horn in on Abagail's discovery.

Mr. O'Keefe, the greens grocer, had perhaps the best motivation of all to attend the dinner. Mrs. O'Keefe said he had to.

One by one the guests arrived at the house of Helmsworth and to inject as much a sense of occasion as possible, formal introductions were extended, wine and h'orderves were served, small talk made and as the clock struck the appropriate hour of eight, dinner was served.

"Professor would you care to say grace?" Bingham offered.

"Oh, I'm not much on prayer Reverend."

"Surely every man, each in his own way, must know how to thank the Lord for our bounty!"

"I think it more appropriate to thank Miss Helmsworth for this Herculean effort!" The others nodded in agreement.

Bingham was not amused.

"Well, if you insist Reverend." All made ready, assumed the position and the Professor prayed.

"Lord we know without a doubt, that you'll bless this food as we pig out! Amen!"

Save for Catherine's giggle, quickly extinguished by Bingham's low growl, silence blanketed the room.

Seconds later, armed with appetites the size of New Hampshire, they attacked the lavishly set table.

It was no accident that Catherine Bingham and Jimmy O'Keefe were seated right next to one another however upon seeing this the good reverend insisted that Catherine change seats to the other side of the table.

Whether by accident or design it happened that the Professor, sitting directly across from young O'Keefe was quick to offer his chair in exchange. Catherine accepted.

Bingham grunted.

Jimmy grinned.

Local heritage having been considered, it was a traditional Pilgrim fare that was thought appropriate and so Abagail had prepared onions quartered and boiled with sugar and raisins on a bed of spinach, boiled pumpkin, boiled Spinach, boiled sweet potatoes and hard brown bread, currants with butter, sugar and vinegar. All the Pilgrim delicacies she could find.

Additionally Abagail had come across an on-line article on sea food the pilgrims might or might not have graced their table with so mackerel, sliced, raw eel and periwinkles with samp were added to the menu.

While most others quietly stared at the alien dishes the professor, now in the middle of the table, graciously heaped his plate with quantities of the unknown foodstuffs while taking his time to peruse and size up his new acquaintances.

"Please be sure to try some of this samp!" Abigail enthusiastically urged as she passed a large bowl of what looked like day old vomit to her guests. "It's the first time I made it!" Abigail proudly boasted.

The boast was unnecessary.

"How adventurous!" Bingham commented.

"What in God's name is samp?" Mr. O'Keefe challenged as he reluctantly peered down into the bowl.

"Hardtack, corn and milk! It's an old, old recipe!" She bragged.

"I can see that!" O'Keefe reinforced.

"Abagail, I must say you've outdone yourself!" Ever the politician Jon Carver complimented.

"Thank Mr. Mayor. For dessert we have prune tart with rosemary, rosewater, cinnamon and sugar. With onions!"

"How delightful!" Quipped Bingham.

It was just about the halfway point through dinner as the Reverend Bingham was passing the still full bowl of samp for its third trip around the table that Catherine excused herself and asked for the ladies room. Abagail quickly volunteered to act as guide and the two left the room.

Minutes later Abagail returned alone unnoticed by all save young Jimmy who was at first puzzled as she softly gesticulated back towards the hall from which she had come. Jimmy was a bit young but not bereft of cope-on and finally nodded in confirmation.

"Ah . . . um . . ." Although not bereft of cope-on, the younger O'Keefe was not old enough to have yet learned how old age and treachery would always overcome youth and enthusiasm and so was not good at conjuring up excuses on short notice.

Abagail again rode to the rescue.

"Jimmy, I completely forgot, didn't you ask me earlier to use the phone to call your coach?"

"Ahhh . . . yes Mr. Helmsworth."

"Jimmy, where's your cell?" His father quickly asked.

"I couldn't find it. I must'a left it home Dad. Sorry."

"It's okay James, he can use my landline. It's just here down the hall Jimmy."

"What do you say Jimmy?" His mother asked as she slid hid I-phone into her purse.

"Thank you Mrs. Helmsworth." Jimmy nearly tripped over himself as he disappeared from the dining room.

"Kids, huh?" Mr. O'Keefe quipped.

Abagail giggled.

Bingham grunted.

"Professor Periwinkle, I do hope you will regale us with some of your exploits!" Abagail prompted.

"Oh you mean the incident with Paul Revere's horse?"

"Amongst others if you are so inclined."

"My pleasure Abigail! The Periwinkels are actually steeped in historical events. It's one of the reasons we have for the last 250 years maintained the pursuit of history as our main undertaking. As a family that is." He explained in between bites still eating as he strategically chewed as he spoke.

"Oh Professor, do please tell us more of further historical adventures of your blood line!" Mrs. Bingham gushed like a school girl at an Elvis concert.

"Oh I don't know that this is the place or the time-"

"It would be an honor professor." Abagail coaxed.

"Well, if you insist. But do you mind if I have some more of that samp first?" Five pairs of hands shot across the table to reach the bowl and pass it to Periwinkle and all stared as he piled the stuff onto his plate next to several slices of raw eel before launching into his story.

"Well, few people know it but, my cousin Shaunaessy had the honor of editing the first draft of the *Brooklyn Address* for President Abraham Lincoln!"

"How exciting!" Mrs. Bingham congratulated. Several guests politely clapped as Abagail glanced around the table.

"The *Brooklyn Address*?" She questioned. "I've done some extensive research on the Lincoln Administration and I don't think I've ever heard of the *Brooklyn Address*." Abigail was compelled to comment.

"You know; 'For score and seven years ago our fathers brought forth on this continent-" Periwinkle started.

"You mean the *Gettysburg Address*!"

"Well that's what the history books call it now but what most people don't know is that it was supposed to be presented at the opening of New York's first Jewish deli on Flatbush Avenue in Brooklyn. Old Abe loved his

38

corned beef and pastrami! But when Lincoln got word of General Meade's victory and how he halted Lee's invasion of the north, my cousin Lenny advised him to travel down to Pennsylvania and make the speech there. And the rest is history!" He triumphantly heralded chewing on an oily piece of eel. "Not something you'd see on the History Channel!"

"Oh." Abagail uttered. The guests stared as Mrs. Bingham clapped.

"It's a very similar situation to how General Waistcoat singlehandedly managed the clearing of The Sahara Forest so the British Army had enough timber to build all those bridges across the Nile and conquer most of North Africa. Including Eqypt."

"Professor, don't you mean the Sahara Desert?" Lester Hickam challenged.

"Yeah, now!"

Everyone quietly returned to pretending to enjoy their dinner.

The good reverend's dismissal of most things scientific aside, no man could accuse him of being a complete dunce and it was only a matter of time until he began to get suspicious as to the whereabouts of Catherine.

The ever alert Abagail noticed what no one else at the table had noticed, namely that Bingham noticed that both his daughter and the O'Keefe boy were now persona non praesenti.

"Professor what do you think this could mean for the library? If you can authenticate our document I mean." The attempted distraction worked, but only temporarily.

"Well Mrs. Helmsworth, should that be the case it's extremely common for a local dignitary, officer or official, in this case Mayor Carver here, to underwrite the authentication stating who found it, when and where. At which time it's normal to submit to the state and then the federal level for research grants to further research the document."

"Er, excuse me Mrs. Helmsworth-"

"Just a second Reverend." Carver interrupted. "What sort of 'grants' Professor?"

"Well, state grants are available of up to twenty, twenty-five thousand dollars while federal grants could reach as high as $100,000."

A second stunned silence swept the room.

"That's an impressive amount!" Carver commented.

"Do a lot'a good in this town!" Councilman Hickam reinforced.

"Excuse me, Abagail-"

"Just a second Reverend. Professor, how exactly will you go about verifying our find?" Abigail pushed.

"Well, it's a multi-step process actually." Periwinkle produced a trifold sheaf of papers. "After I've examined the document and sent a small piece of the parchment off to the MIT labs for dating and consulted the Harvard Stacks I'll issue a detailed report of my findings. These," He passed the papers to Craver, "will allow you, Mayor Carver to co-sign or grant permission of the locals to enter into a business arrangement concerning the document while acting as a co-signer to verify how any money will be spent."

It was at that point that the good reverend decided the bounds of etiquette had been reached and the Marquis of Queensbury rules no longer applied and so he pushed away from the table, got up and marched out of the room to head down the hall where he found what he wasn't looking for: his beloved Catherine and young Jimmy locked in each other's arms engaged in the most passionate game of tonsil hockey anyone had ever seen.

Abagail, sensing the impending squall, stood to signal the dinner had ended. The remainder of the guests followed suite and it was then that an interesting series of sounds emanated from the back hallway up into the dining room.

Each guest would later render an opinion as to exactly what was happening unseen by all but the three parties involved but most agreed that there was a masculine roar followed by a fist hitting some part of the anatomy, most likely a jaw, followed by a grunt, a feminine scream, and a thud to the floor.

Whatever the theoretical occurrence of events all agree on what followed.

Catherine ran crying from the house, the Reverend Bingham appeared, was slapped across the face by Mrs. Bingham who stormed out and the dinner was formally over.

A minute later young Jimmy O'Keefe came stumbling out into the dining room rubbing his chin.

"Kids!" Mr. O'Keefe shook his head as he poured another glass of wine.

"Professor, perhaps we can meet over at the library in the morning and I can show you the document? I've set aside a space in the research room for you and have found a volunteer to assist you for anything you might need."

"You are a most gracious host Miss Helmsworth, I look forward to our meeting tomorrow." He said as he kissed her hand. She blushed. "Abagail, do mind if take some of the leftover samp home?"

"I'll just fetch a Tupperware container foe you." She offered.

The Phone Call
†

Abigail Helmsworth had no way of knowing that the morning after the dinner, while she was dutifully fulfilling her duties over at the Herman Melville Memorial Library, Councilman Lester Hickam was fulfilling his assigned duties over at the city council chambers/firehouse and police station when he was compelled to ring over to Jon Carver, P-town's mayor who was fulfilling his sworn obligations over in his hardware store on Commercial Street. As was his habit he was doing so with his feet propped up on his desk perusing the *Boston Globe* while enjoying a cup of coffee, milk no sugar.

Just as he turned the page to the Classifieds Jon released a loud grunt when he had to reach over and pick up the phone on the third ring.

"Hardware. Carver here."

"Jon?"

"Mormin' Lester. What's the matter?"

There were only three times in their twenty-six year friendship that Lester rang Jon before eleven in the morning on a weekday.

Eighteen years ago after the birth of his son Edgar Allen, sixteen years ago when Hurricane Jehoshaphat was on her way in and ten and a half years back when some British sailors on shore leave stumbled into Jimmy Kelly's bar over on Cornwell, found out he didn't serve Smithwick's Ale only Guinness and a donnybrook broke out. Didn't end too well for the two Brits the sheriff and the medics carried out of the place. The other two limped out behind propped up on each other.

"Well Jon, I think all's okay but I thought I should give you a quick call."

Jon put his feet down and sat up in his chair.

"I reiterate Lester, what's the matter?"

"Well . . . you know how much this document thing means to Abagail-"

"Lester what did you do?"

"Now Jon don't go getting' angry but they called me, I didn't call them! I mean they called and I got all worked up and couldn't think of anything else to say!"

"Who called? Called about what?"

"Jon I just . . . I just had to say yes! I mean, I couldn't say no now could I?!"

"They who?!"

"*The Boston Globe*. They want to send a reporter and someone else out here to do a story on the papers Abagail found.

"Someone else like who Lester?"

"A . . . a camera crew." He squeaked into the phone. "A small one."

"Since when do newspapers come with camera crews?"

"Promise you won't yell at me Jon." Lester heard only silence coming from the other end of the line. "Jon, you there Jon?"

"Lester you do know what day it is don't you?"

"Jon I –"

"In less than 24 hours traffic is gonna be backed up all the way down the Cape and we are gonna be inundated with twenty to thirty thousand tourists wanting to cram in here and that's just the tip of the iceberg! It'll be upwards of sixty thousand by Sunday, half of 'em drunk off their heads!"

"But Jon, we ain't never had no trouble, no real trouble on the Fourth before! In fact it's our biggest source of income, the tourists."

"I ain't talkin' about anything to do with tourist income! I'm talkin' about how's it gonna look us finding the oldest deed to possibly the oldest **church** in all of New England with guys dressed in skirts, high heels, wigs and make-up! parading through the streets all weekend?!"

"Well . . . I reckon the Catholics wouldn't have too many objections to it."

"No but there is another problem. Bingham's church ain't Catholic now is it!?"

"But Jon-"

"And another thing. What'a we do if it turns out it ain't authentic and the whole U.S Press corps is here to report it?! Look pretty stupid then, don't ya think? We'd end up the punch line to a joke fer Christ's sake!"

"Jon I –"

"You remember the headache we had with the Reverend, the LONESOME's and that bus load'a girls from the Young Women's Christian Association from out in Brockton when Frank and his volunteers had to clean up those four dozen condoms all along the shore a couple'a years back?"

"It was five dozen Jon."

"HOW MANY AIN'T THE POINT NUMBNUTS!"

"Sorry Jon."

"Frank said his guys were out there on South Beach next morning for half the day fer cryin'n out loud!"

"Now fair's fair Jon, half them prophylactics those girls brought with them!" Jon ignored the detail and ranted on.

"Not to mention the Health Inspector once the State Board of Health caught wind of what went on."

"Went **in's** more like!" He joked.

"IT AIN'T FUNNY LESTER!"

"Sorry Jon. Just tryin' to lighten' the mood."

There was another ominously long silence on the phone.

"Jon? You still there?"

"Alright then. Maybe I can convince them to sit on the story until the morning edition of the Fourth after we get the Professor's report!"

Even the great Jon Carver was of limited power and influence and by that Friday morning the story reached Reuter's. By noon it had gone national and by two fifteen NYU, BU and Yale had all contacted the town council informing them that they intended to send teams of archaeologists up to examine the document and to arrange a dig around the church for other items.

Abagail and the LONESOME's were not too keen on that idea until informed if anything of any significance were found it could lead to an additional sizeable government grant for the town coffers, some cash from each of the Ivy League schools involved as well as a trust fund set up by the Commonwealth at which point they got pretty excited.

Until they were cautioned it could also spell trouble by the way of law suits at which point they became worried until they were also informed the amount of money, six figures, at which point they got excited again.

Of course there was always the possibility that the document could be claimed by the State under the Commonwealth's laws of Immanent Domain which again made them scared.

But the town lawyers reckoned that if enough public awareness was raised, all'd probably be okay.

Probably.

The Reverend Bingham Goes to Confession
†

Charged with the Christian guilt that made America great, Cecil approached Catherine as she stood in the garden glancing out across the beach and off into the afternoon distance.

He cleared his throat several times as he approached her from behind but was duly ignored.

She stood fast and didn't react.

"Tea's ready Cat." He quietly announced. She folded her arms. "The sea is lovely this time of year, don't you think?"

She grunted.

Ahh, progress! He mused to himself. He drew up behind her, folded his arms and stared down at the grass.

"Catherine I-"

"Dad . . ."

"Yes dear?"

"What were they like?"

"Who?"

"My real parents."

"We are you're real parents Catherine."

"My biological parents."

"Oh, well. . . I don't really know. We never met them or any other of your relatives. The orphanage forbids release of all related family data unless requested by the offspring." A long silence ensued. "Do you want to contact the orphanage and research your biological parents?" He prayed not as the Binghams never told Cat about the accident. In fact had never talked about her birth parents save for the fact that they were teachers who had to give her up for adoption.

"No. No. I owe you and mother everything."

"We love you."

"I know. And I love you both, very much." He

46

ventured one step closer and took her hand.

"I called into the O'Keefe's this morn-"

"YOU WHAT!?" Bingham immediately realized he'd thrown for an interception. "FATHER IS IT YOUR LIFE'S MISSION TO HUMILIATE ME BEYOND ALL REDEMTION?"

"Cath, I-"

"BAD ENOUGH YOU ATTACK THE ONE BOY WHO NOTICES ME AT SCHOOL!! NOW I-"

"TO APOLOGIZE!" Stunned beyond speech Catherine's anger quickly evaporated as she stumbled back and stared.

In all her eighteen years as a Bingham she had never heard her father utter the whisper of a hint of an apology for anything, including the time in the pulpit when he mistakenly attributed John 3:34 to Ecclesiastes 7:12.

"You . . . you what?"

"I apologized, face-to-face with young Jimmy."

"How did he take it?"

"Well . . . like a man!" It was Catherine's turn to move closer. "Like an upright and magnanimous man of truth and bearing."

"Dad . . . they were teachers, you told me that much, and that was their life, whatever that life was. You and mother have your life. Now it's time for me to be allowed my life."

"But –"

"And either you trust me to make the right choices or you don't and I hope that you do. But-"

"Catherine, we trust-"

"But if you don't, I shall have to learn the hard way. But when it comes right down to it, you have to know that I would never do anything to embarrass you and mother!"

"Catherine, it's not just that you're our only daughter, child, you have to understand that it's all through those first long years of our marriage when we

47

were faced with the prospect of growing old together with no children, much less grandchildren that . . ."

"I get it." Again he took her by the hand.

"Alright, look here. Never let it be said that Cecil T. Bingham stood in the way of true love."

Charged with joy Catherine spun around to face her father.

"Does that mean I can go to the dance?"

"I'll instruct your mother to take you into Cape Cod this afternoon and find a dress appropriate for a young woman of such sound judgment. One that can be trusted to strike out on her own and make her parents proud!" She leaned in and kissed him hard on the cheek. "There's one condition!" He added. Catherine froze.

"As long as he asks you! I'm adamant about that. No daughter of mine is gonna earn the title of hussy before she's twenty!"

"Oh Daddy! You've made me-" He put his finger to her lips.

"Mother's waiting, go and have your tea."

She squealed before running off into the house.

Knowing he hit a home run Cecil, hands in pockets, strolled back into the house to have his tea quoting Ecclesiastes. This time correctly.

"For it is written that wisdom is as good as an inheritance, yea better!"

The Big Day

†

From behind their barricades the Yankees fired a healthy volley of musket fire. Smoke obscured much of the battleground but the redcoats assembled at the foot of the small hill marched bravely forward, undeterred and yet to open to fire. The Americans, at least the Americans pretending to be colonists, bravely manned their trenches, reloaded and once again took aim at the cursed Redcoats, that is the Americans pretending to be Redcoats, who for their part strode on as if each man knew wouldn't die that day.

At the front of the large semi-circle of abut fifty men, all decked out in their smart colonial blue, was General William Prescott, the Colonial colors flying high above him as once again the Colonial muskets made ready,

At the foot of the small hill, the old Union Jack flapping in the breeze, General Gage stood on one side with William Howe and another hundred men between them. In reality there were only about 47 men but nobody questioned the free tourist brochure they had been given earlier that morning.

Bill Mitchell head of the volunteer fire brigade kept most of his men on close standby should a musket spark ignite the dry grass surrounding the Pilgrim Monument. Later that evening they would be called on to man the fireworks display.

Formed in three perfect ranks of six men it was with military discipline they waited until the final order was given.

"TROOP ADVANCE!" Ordered Gage and the Redcoats advanced.

Musket fire was duly exchanged, several combatants on both sides gave award winning death scenes and everybody clapped.

Pilgrim's Hill is only about ninety-eight feet high but it served the purpose and in in P-town they called that purpose The Battle of Bunker Hill. The Battle of Pilgrim Monument didn't have much of a ring to it.

All the town's folk backed by as many of the out-of-towners they could squeeze into the square had gathered around High Pole Road surrounding the Pilgrim Monument to watch the short but epic battle but, now that, to everyone's relief America would be free for another year as it ended in another Continental victory, the mob disbursed and headed to the main street to watch the parade and listen to the speeches which this year would prove to be little different.

The big announcement, rumors of which had been circulating ever since that Harvard Professor came to town, were expected to be confirmed today. To wit that P-town was perhaps home to the only U.S. church established by George Washington himself!

The official launch point was on Bradford Street and the short route was doubled by looping around at the end of Commercial Street and marching back to the start point.

Following the heroic taking of Bunker Hill by the friendly forces the town parade started promptly at eleven a.m. which itself would stretch on into 11:27 allowing the visitors to be crammed into P-town square like 60,000 sardines where, at 12 noon sharp a collection of dignitaries would speak.

The Mayor, accompanied by the governor and his usual entourage, made their way towards the town center where the main review stand would mark the official end of the parade to make the monumental announcement to the world and award the town their officially sanctioned, ornamented building plaque and what all were certain would improve the town's sagging, off peak tourist trade.

It was full steam ahead for the grandest gala since July 4th, 1776 as the locals would forgo any semblance of a normal routine in order to focus all efforts on the upcoming celebration.

✝

The fateful moment arrived and the small reviewing stand in the town square, made ready the night before, was strategically positioned directly under the large Carver's Hardware sign and it podium sat behind The V.I.P.'s red, white and blue draped stage. A small, ten wooden folding chairs served as a grand stand and the townsfolk gathered.

The head count of dignitaries, The Governor and his entourage, the Mayor his wife and his two man entourage of the head councilman and secretary along with Abagail being watched over by Higgins, were all present and accounted for at the assigned place and time.

All that is except Periwinkle.

The parade trickled to an end and it was time to start the speech making.

Following the requisite political rhetoric by the Governor, the congratulatory kudos by the Mayor and a few lame excuses for the delay as they waited for the professor to show up, Carver stepped away from the mike.

"Where's this damn professor?"

Meanwhile, back at the library office, as if he were playing a mini-game of Whack-a-Mole, Professor Periwinkle was furiously banging away on his keyboard, rushing to get his official report typed up in time to have a private conference with the LONESOME's before the big announcement by the Governor scheduled for twenty minutes ago.

"Abagail! Where's this damn professor?" An worried Mayor repeated as he paced. A nervous Abagail shrugged, and an annoyed Reverend Bingham harrumphed.

As if on cue an excited Periwinkle appeared down the street awkwardly jogging up the sidewalk like a wolf with one leg in trap waving a sheaf of papers above his head. He made his way through the throng and breathlessly sought out the Mayor at the back of the small stage.

"Where the hell you been Periwinkle!" Carver quietly demanded.

Due to some vital reference material from Harvard having only arrived that morning there was no time to finish his report and pre-brief the Mayor as planned who in turn was to brief the governor prior to him making the much anticipated announcement to the gathered masses.

"We need to talk Your Honor." Jon immediately picked up on the bad vibe and took control.

"Abagail? Abagail!" He quietly yelled so as to not alert the noisy crowd.

"What?!"

"Get up there and tell the folks about how you found the document."

"What, again? I just told them not ten minutes go!"

"Well then tell them about the historical significance of the find!"

"I told them that too! Besides it's all anybody's been talking about in this town for the past four days. They've been talking about it more than all those Senate investigations! They know full well what the historical significance is!"

"Well then tell 'em a damn joke or about George Washington's false teeth or something! Anything, just buy us a little time till we get our shit together back here!"

A nervous Abagail again stepped up to the mike and combed her brain for material with which to filibuster.

"What the hell's going on Periwinkle? Give me that

report so the governor can make this big announcement." Carver demanded.

"I don't think that's such a good idea Mr. Mayor."

"Why in the hell not?" Just then the Governor's head popped into the conversation.

"So this must be the distinguished Professor. Very nice to meet you Dr. Periwinkle. Have you got this all-important report?"

"Well, yes Governor but I don't think you want to-"

"With all due respect gentlemen, I've get five more of these shindigs to get to today and my helicopter is standing by down on the beach. So let's have it."

"Sir, you might want to read through it first." Periwinkle advised.

"Bull puckey Boy! I make these malarkey laced speeches on the run for a living! Give it here."

"But Governor-" The Governor grabbed the report and made his way up the few steps to the stage.

It was with much pomp and little circumstance the governor took to the podium and brandished a smile rivaling that of the Cheshire Cat.

"Uh, ladies and gentlemen, and those of you who are undecided . . ." He nodded down at a group of gaily dressed gays in the crowd who waved their rainbow flags, lifted their appletinis and laughed at his reference.

"It is a privilege and an honor to be invited here today to address you lovely folks of Provincetown. May I compliment the town fathers on the lovely decorations, procedures and effort they put into this Independence Day celebration." More applause followed.

"What exactly's in that report Professor?" Carver pushed.

Periwinkle nervously glanced about, drew closer to the Mayor and whispered in his ear.

The Mayor's eyes shot wide open and, being a former Navy man, again immediately took control. He dashed up the short ladder in back of the stage and leaned into the Governor and whispered to him just as he begun to speak.

The Governor's eyes shot wide open and, being a former Army man he immediately realized he had to pass the buck. He perused the colorful crowd and quickly changed tone as he immediately realized the potential political repercussions of what he had just been told. He stepped back to the mike.

With the burden of the awful news he had just been given now off his shoulders Jon Carver breathed a deep sigh of relief and relaxed and returned to his seat.

"But to be honest, something I know you're probably not used to hearing from a politician!" A dramatic pause was had to allow the proper ripple of laughter. "I've just been informed of how long you've been waiting to hear this potentially spectacular news and I feel it is my sworn duty to allow the privilege of releasing this all-important news concerning your local church to your good mayor. Mayor Carver, would you step to the podium please?"

Jon, who had been perusing the sports page he held low at his side was startled. His wife nudged him and reluctantly he dropped the newspaper and made his way to the microphone. The governor continued to slither out of the situation.

"I feel honor bound to do this because it wouldn't be right of me to steal anybody's thunder. And I'm on a tight schedule to get back to Boston, so without further delay I'd like to ask the honorable Jon Carver here to take the mike and give you the good news! Jon step over here!"

Taken completely off guard and like Gort the robot it was with a blank stare that Jon Carver mechanically took the folder from the Governor and peered out over the crowd.

"Well, my helicopter is waiting down on South Beach so I need to run." The Governor tagged his comments. "I wish the folks of P-town a great Fourth of July, and don't forget, vote Democrat!" To tempestuous applause the big man scurried down the steps and, body guards flanking him on either side, disappeared into the crowd.

Gort had now turned into a zombie in a George Romero movie as Mayor Carver continued to gaze out over the crowd, immobile while his mind raced for an escape exit.

"GET ON WITH IT!" Someone in the crowd finally yelled out.

"COME ON JON! WE GOT SOME SERIOUS DRINIKNG TO DO! GIVE US THE GOOD NEWS ALREADY!" A second heckler joined in. Aggravated by the heat of the midday sun murmurs permeated the crowd.

Suddenly Carver remembered his political superpower – bullshitting!

"Well, looks like what we found out was -" He paused and feigned a contemplative moment. "Ya know what?! I think the good news, carefully uncovered by the meticulous work of a very diligent, hardworking individual by rights should be . . ."

Abagail blushed in her seat on the reviewing stand. At the same time over his shoulder Jon happened to spy Periwinkle slinking back through the crowd. Carver quickly signaled to a nearby pugnacious deputy to hold the professor where he was and the big cop complied.

"At this time I would like to call to the podium the person who made this all possible." Abagail demurely rose to her feet and started toward the podium only to pump the brakes as the Mayor continued. "Professor Periwinkle step up here sir!" Periwinkle froze in place but was quickly shoved forward by the deputy.

The crowd cheered, Carver smiled and Abagail was miffed as Periwinkle's diminutive frame was forcibly escorted through the crowd, up the stairs and to the

Mayor. Jon encouraged the crowd to greet him with more energetic applause.

Jon handed the Professor back the report, patted the small man on the back and made his way back to his seat.

Holding his old brown leather briefcase tight to his chest, mostly as a prop, it was an embarrassed and unprepared Periwinkle that stepped over to the podium, sneered at Carver and approached the mike.

With the TV cameras rolling, the fireworks standing by and the townsfolk holding their collective breath he spoke what he was certain would be his own epitaph.

"Hi." He meekly peeped into the microphone.

"HI YERSELF! YOU GOT SOMETHING TO TELL US OR WHAT PROFESSOR?!"

"Uh . . . uh, yes. Yes I do. He thrust a hand into his satchel and produced a sheaf of papers which he laid on the podium and quickly perused through. "Uhh . . . after much due diligence and extensive research, with the uh . . . dedicated staff of your local archivist —" Abagail crossed her arms, looked away and grunted. I came across a very complete history of your . . . ah quaint little church.

The crowd quieted and Reverend Bingham who had been slumped down between Abagail and his wife, nodding on and off, was elbowed in the ribs and suddenly sat up.

"The old building at 127 Alden Road, now Pastor Bingham's Eighth Day Adventist church, is authenticated to have been built in 1775, just as the War for Independence was launched." Wild cheering broke out across the square and Periwinkle was encouraged. "It indeed did start life in Revolutionary times not as a church, but as a sort of comfort station for the weary soldiers of General Washington's Continental Army." More clapping followed.

"127 Alden Road it appears was a popular haunt and

a place of rest and relaxation for the exhausted farmers and soldiers fighting the great struggle of the American Revolution against the English in 1776. Perhaps even the very place where prominent leaders plotted the very struggle which led to America's freedom." Several in the crowd shushed the rest to hear all the juicy details. Periwinkle now read from his notes.

"Closed from the end of the Revolution until the mid-Nineteenth Century there's no record of its official use again until the onset of our entry into the Great War in 1917. On December eighth, 1941 by order of William Franklin Knox Secretary of the Navy the abandoned building at 127 Alden Road was commandeered by the U.S. Coast Guard and redesigned as a lookout post and quarters for the six man swift boat/PT boat squad CG Patrol 14 tasked with keeping lookout for German submarines."

Several former Marines and a couple of the gays, former Air Force, in the crowd hooted loudly.

"However, its original purpose at that time was still unknown. Through contacts at the Harvard stacks I was able to locate documents tracing ownership back to Mrs. Helmsworth's discovered documents in 1775." People clapped as he turned back and gestured to Abagail who uncrossed her arms, forced a smile at him and nodded.

"They for the most part were papers related to some legal transactions after the death of King George and so postdate the Revolution however, the one irrefutable piece of information I was able to uncover-" More fumbling of notes ensued. ". . . in both the Harvard Stacks and the Commonwealth's birth records reinforced by the parish church and tax records of the period, was that the original structure was built as a going business concern when the existing business grew too large for the small two room premises already in full swing at the outbreak of hostilities with England in early 1776."

"JUMPIN' JEHOSAPHATS PROFFESSOR! THE

NEXT WAR'LL BE IN FULL SWING BY THE TIME YOU GET TO THE POINT!"

"YEAH PROF! EXACTLY WHAT THE HELL YOU GETTING' AT?"

"I'm getting there, I'm getting there! The business was under the control of a one Marie de Coultier."

"WELL WHO THE HECK WAS SHE WHEN SHE WAS HOME?!" Periwinkle sensed the crowd growing ugly.

"It appears the business was a . . . I don't speak French so pardon my pronunciation here, but her profession was listed as a Maison de putain."

Down in the crowd a middle-aged couple stood listening intently. "Oh they made Mason jars! My grandma used to use those to can peaches! How sweet."

"Agnes shut up will ya?!" Her husband snapped.

"The last short paragraph of this letter found with the document is not actually in lawyerese as originally thought but in old French. But as I said I don't speak French and there wasn't enough time to get it translated –"

Carver nudged his son sitting next to him.

"Jimmy, didn't you take some French back in high school?"

"Yeah but just to get girls." O'Keefe reached over and smacked his son Jimmy in back of the head.

"Go help the man out, Bonehead!"

Jimmy O'Keefe approached the reviewing stand took the letter from the professor and read it aloud.

"à ma main ce trentième jour de juin, dans l'année de notre Seigneur, 1775. By my hand this thirtieth day of June in the year of our Lord, 1775, signed Marie la Putain."

"What the heck is a Mason de la repatition?" Bingham called out from his seat.

Jimmy answered back into the microphone.

"A Maison de mauvaise rèputation. A Maison de la

58

Prostitution. The old church was a brothel."

"COME AGAIN JIMMY?!" Someone called out.

"YOU TRYIN' TO TELL US THAT REVEREND BINGHAM'S CHURCH WAS A WHOREHOUSE?"

A deadly silence fell over the crowd.

"Well now I wouldn't exactly say –"

"HOLY SHIT! BINGHAM'S CHURCH WAS A WHOREHOUSE?" One of the gays gleefully exclaimed.

Bingham felt his knees weaken just before he slumped over into his wife's lap and passed out.

The wild cheering, jeering and hollering that ensued rivaled anything that occurred on VE Day.

Young Jimmy fought back a smirk as he glanced down into the crowd and made eye contact with Catherine who covered her mouth to hide her giggling.

The Aftermath

†

It was on the front steps of 127 Alden that Reverend Bingham sat, head in hands, desperately searching his mind for what purpose could the Lord have had, in His mysterious yet infinite wisdom to have bestowed this curse upon his most loyal and humble servant.

Devastated by the news that his house of worship was once a house of ill repute Cecil at first flew into a rage declaring it was a lie no doubt instigated by the Jews or worse yet – the Papists.

After realizing there were no Jews in P-town, save for the Birnbaums now in their eighties and the few Catholics there were didn't practice anymore he was left with no choice but to face the facts.

But he wasn't going to take it lying down! He vowed to fight it, all the way to the Supreme Court if need be!

"But Cecil, the Supreme Court can only change the law, it can't change the facts." His faithful wife consoled, offering a hot cup of lemon tea before taking a seat on the step next to him.

"Besides Cecil, maybe this is The Lord's way of telling you that it's alright if Catherine wants to date the O'Keefe boy."

"What?! Now it's insult to injury is it?"

"He's not such a bad boy! Doesn't drink, doesn't smoke and from what I hear doing quite well at university out in Boston."

"He ain't in Boston! He's only out in Worcester!"

Realizing Cecil had to decompress at his own pace, Myrtel passed him his tea.

"I've a suggestion for Sunday's sermon, if you're interested." She demurely offered.

Realizing there were no grounds to be angry at the woman who had stood by him for the last thirty plus years Bingham softened his stance

"Yes dear. What is it?"

"You can explain to your flock how even the most vile place such as this structure once was, can find salvation and by the will of God be transformed into a house of worship."

Cecil smiled and nodded.

"I think I like that." He leaned over and kissed her on the cheek. "I would be a lost sheep without you!"

Mrs. Bingham gave him a peck on the forehead, got up and walked back across the garden to the house.

After a discerning minute Cecil looked over his shoulder, produced a flask and spilled a meager amount of Glenn Fiddich into his tea. He lifted the cup and looked up to God.

"Oh well . . . I suppose at least it brought people together. Make love not war, eh?!" He toasted the heavens.

✝

Due to what they considered 'the lurid nature' of the document Abagail did not get her discovery endorsed by the State of Massachusetts. When word of this reached the Press Christie Ann Hefner immediately called an emergency meeting of the *Playboy* board of trustees.

Hustler and *Big Uns*, joined by several other men's magazines were quick to climb on board and together the publishers donated 1.5 million to Abagail's library.

News of the donation made national headlines which sparked public outcry against the state's decision not to verify the deed and it was only a matter of a couple of weeks before a special delivery letter reached Abagail's office informing her that the head of the State Historical Society, Michael O'Callaghan, who just happened to be running for the senate at the time, had reconsidered the earlier decision.

Oddly enough, Abigail eventually got her document not only certified by the state but by the feds too. As soon as the distinguished Dr. David J. Skorton Director of the Smithsonian Institute caught wind of Abigail's discovery he not only invited her to speak before the institute's annual convention but authorized a grant to establish a Herman Melville Library Trust Fund for the preservation of rare books and documents.

Of course explaining the purpose of the deed and what 127 Alden Road was originally built for was judiciously circumvented in Abigail's address to the institute's members, an address entitled, "They Weren't All Minute Men". It was simply referred to as an 'R & R' station.

Doris Needlebaum's *Curl Up & Dye Beauty Salon* sued about the space they had to give up when the ground work for the new building commenced but when Abigail agreed to give her a corner in the gift shop of the museum, all was forgiven and she dropped the suit.

That Autumn Jimmy O'Keefe and young Catherine got an apartment in Worcester so Jimmy could finish off his degree. There was considerable stress on the young household when Cecil Bingham threatened to cut off and disown Catherine who had enrolled in nursing school.

That is until word reached them that there was a New York writer with a film producer attached who was interested in optioning their young couple's story rights for a romantic comedy. Bingham sat sternly monitoring the meeting with the producer but ultimately endorsed all the production company's terms.

As for Professor Emiratis Jubile Q. Periwinkle, Ph.D. and Mrs. Hannah Higgins, they left on a spontaneous vacation a month ago and haven't been heard from since.

Abagail was sure to apply a fresh coat of Brasso brass polish every day to the official landmark plaque which hung to the right of the main entrance of the

Herman Melville Memorial Library. And *The Boston Globe* gave the residents of P-town, New England a full front page story and everything seemed to work out fine.

Of course there's still the problem of most of the tourists being siphoned off by that other town. You know, the one with the witches.

THE END

Dr. Lindsay's Christmas

To all the children of the world who keep the spirit of
Christmas alive in their hearts.

The Event

It is difficult to fathom the depths of another's depression. To know to what depths is he willing to descend to assuage his pain. Simple anger? Expensive counseling? Rum, rye, whiskey or other over-the-counter pharmaceuticals?

Perhaps even to the ultimate act of self-absorption suicide?

There are those who ultimately arrive at a place where they begin to doubt all they once held to be true. A place in time and space where all points of reference merge into one and evaporate.

For the lover it can be betrayal by a partner.

For a businessman it's the moment when his lawyer's inform him of the fine print he overlooked on a multi-millin dollar contract.

For a presidential candidate it's the moment the FBI discovers she has lied about some e-mails.

All these suppositions of course are merely variables. However, given exponential expansion, they inevitably lead to one certainty. Somewhere, somehow a solution has to present itself.

Doctor Jonathan Michael Lindsay inadvertently arrived at that point shortly before midnight on Christmas Eve, nineteen hundred and eighty-seven.

Lindsay came into the world in an upstairs bedroom at number 17 Merchant's Quay, Dublin, Ireland only seconds after midnight on the first of January, in the year of our Lord 1900, officially making him the first baby born in King Edward's provinces of Great Britain and

Ireland at the turn of the millennium. A place the English mistakenly referred to as the United Kingdom.

Many things had transpired in the intervening 87 years of Lindsay's long and healthy life.

Having been raised in a God fearing Catholic family and having been imbued with a strong work ethic, it was through academics and intellect that Jonathan rose quickly through the social ranks of 20th Century Irish society.

A solicitor uncle in Dublin provided young Jonathan with an escape from the European Troubles of war as the English fought the Kaiser and the Irish fought to escape the English. This was accomplished by securing the young man an appointment to the Irish Royal College of Surgeons where he graduated with honors.

In the Twenties, with a small loan, Jonathan was able to set up a modest medical practice on the south side of the capital and it was only a matter of time until he took Mary Gormley from Wexford as his wife. Many said that it was in part due to the fact that the couple could not have children that Jonathan drifted into pediatrics where he spent the remainder of his life treating the children of Rathgar, Blackrock, Rathmines and anywhere else his two door, four cylinder Benson motorcar could carry him.

As one would expect money was never an object for Jonathan particularly when it came to his sworn duty, even refusing to retire after the unfortunate demise of Mary, whose grave he visited without fail every Sunday after mass to set flowers at her headstone out in Glasnevin.

As was his irreconcilable nature, he did this come rain or shine.

In time he adjusted to the absence of her voice, the song of her laughter and long gone were the days that he, along with Mary and sometimes friends, would hike out to the foothills of the Wicklow Mountains on a weekend picnic.

Now, bent with age but still with full wits about him, the O'Connell Bridge to the Parnell Monument and back was about all he could manage in one go. But the five or six block journey was enough to ease his creeping depression.

Such was the case this Thursday evening.

Death Knocks

It was cold but dry and the last minute shopping chaos which was the Dublin City Centre had begun to subside. It was Christmas Eve and the wide street was adorned with holiday lights from the river all the way north as far as could be seen. The shops likewise were dressed out in celebration of the highest high holy day of the Christian calendar.

Down on the Southside the good doctor had closed up clinic early and taken the trolley into town to get something to eat. He disembarked at Westmoreland Street and, through the dark and light wind he hiked over the O'Connell Bridge. There he crossed in front of the Four Provinces statue. O'Connell Street, well known for its fine display of statues, reminded Jonathan of many of the grander European boulevards he and Mary had visited in their time together. He took his usual path, the path he had unconsciously established five or six weeks ago after Mary's funeral mass at St. Andrew's in Blackrock.

As he strolled past Eason's book shop and then the GPO he tipped his hat in remembrance of the brave men and women who died that week back when he was just sixteen years of age.

By the time he crossed Parnell Street at the north end of O'Connell and began the return journey south past The Gresham Hotel, the evening's ambulation had worked its magic. His melancholia had begun to dissipate.

As he reached the gaily decorated show windows of Clery's department store his mind wandered to the happier times with his wife and he was near wholly

72

lifted from his dark mood.

Old Man Clery traditionally made it a point to outdo all the other shops in the City Centre with the entire building, the largest on the boulevard, wrapped in a giant ribbon and a bow of dancing lights while the oversized display windows were a buzz of activity. In an idyllic parlor setting a family of mannequins robotically feigned a family exchanging gifts on Christmas morning. A train set circled the base of the large, gaily decorated pine tree which disappeared up into the ceiling of the window and behind it a pointy hatted elf peeked in through the garden window. Christmas carols emanated from exterior speakers.

Several people were gathered at the bus stop outside the sprawling storefront and Jonathan glanced up at the landmark, triple faced clock which read 6:37 p.m. He fought back a smile as he glanced across the street to Eason's clock, directly opposite Clery's and noted their clock claimed it to be 6:40.

Like the Dublin cathedrals Christ Church and St. Patrick's, no two ever agreed.

A group of shoppers to include a little boy and his father, a little girl in a new wool coat and pristine red hat accompanied by her mother and an old woman on her own were staring into the colorfully lit, elaborate window display. Several others hovered at the bus stop behind them. Lindsay drank in the scene.

The boy and the girl gazed into the window watching the marionettes. The parents attempted to keep the children's attention, but they were too mesmerized by the Christmas display and bounced around with the anticipation of the coming evening.

"Mummy, if we had a time machine could we keep going back in time and have Christmas every day?" The little girl asked.

"Yes Sweetie, we could. But sure what would you do with all those Barbie dolls?"

Jonathan made his way around them and set off in search of some supper. Shunning several offers of Christmas Eve dinner he would wait to deal with his friends and their families in the morning.

"Da, why does Santie always wear red?" The small boy pried.

"Because it's bright and cheerful."

"Does that mean the Devil is bright and cheerful too?"

"You're your mother's child! Come along, we have to get up to the hotel to meet ya ma, if we're late they'll be the Devil to pay!."

As they turned away from the window the boy lost control of his ball and it bounced down the path into the lay-by of the bus stop out in the street.

"I'll get it!" The little girl enthusiastically called out as she was already in pursuit of the toy.

Her mother, rummaging through her purse for bus change, heard only a shrill scream followed by the horrible screech of brakes, a nauseating thud and the deafening blast of a bus horn. The mother turned and the little girl lay motionless, half sprawled under the bus. A morbid silence swept the onlookers.

Following an eternity of stillness Lindsay scurried to the unconscious child pulling off his fedora and heavy coat as he dashed as best he could.

"Move, move! Make way! You, I need help!" The man he chose dashed to Jonathan's aid.

"Kneel here! Hold her head. Keep it in line with her body, she may have a cervical injury. No matter what happens don't let her head move, you understand?!"

"Yes sir." The man became an automaton. Sounds of traffic screeching and horns honking filled the back ground as rubber-neckers slowed by the scene.

"Don't let her head move!" Jonathan's face drained to white when, in the light if the department store window, he saw both her eyes were darkening.

"Madam, I'll need that gift box. You, raise her legs and hold them up. Somebody give me a scarf! Does anyone have a mobile?"

A woman moved to comfort the hysterical mother. The bus driver sat on the bus step, face-in-hands, on the verge of tears unable to speak.

As Lindsay took the wrapped gift box from the woman everyone in the crowd, to include the Little Boy, produced a mobile and offered them to him.

"Someone call emergency services." They all began to punch buttons.

"Only one!" He yelled as he worked.

Lindsay quickly fashioned a cervical collar from the cardboard and carefully applied it to his young patient holding it in place with the scarf. Unable to locate a pulse he issued more orders.

"Okay, ease her head down. Can you do CPR?" The dumfounded man nodded yes.

"Be sure to cover her mouth and nose. And for God's sake don't exhale to hard or you'll damage the bronchiolli, I'll apply closed cardiac. One breath every five compressions. Ready? One, two, three, four five. Breath!"

They worked feverishly on the child for what seemed to be an eternity, Lindsay intermittently checking her vital signs. Then, as suddenly as it all began, it stopped.

"Doctor, her nose is bleeding!" The man noted. Her tiny nose began to hemorrhage fluid and blood and the orbits around her eyes were completely dark.

Jonathan slowly looked up, and then over to the window display. The robots mockingly smiled back at him.

"Are you a doctor?" One of the by-standers asked.

"No I'm the fickin' traffic warden!" Jonathan slowly struggled to his feet and made his way through the small crowd and to the side of the department store to lean against the wall. A Garda came jogging down the street and recognized Lindsay.

"Doctor Lindsay, can you tell me what happened?" The young Garda asked. Lindsay stared back blankly.

"Hit. Hit by the bus."

"And . . . is she?"

"Look at her eyes. Two black eyes, nasal hemorrhage. Basal skull fracture. She never had a chance."

"What shall I list as the official time of death sir?" He manned his official Garda note pad as a second policeman was covering the girl's corpse with Lindsay's overcoat.

"Christmas time."

"Sir, I have to do a report-"

"YOU HAVE A WATCH HAVEN'T YA?! List it as too soon!"

Lindsay staggered away from the scene and around the corner.

"Sorry for your troubles doctor."

"I didn't know her." He called back.

"Not the child sir. Your wife." Ignoring the Garda he staggered away.

Rounding the corner Lindsay braced himself against the side wall of the cathedral. Nausea slowly crept over him until he could no longer fight it off. He vomited into a rubbish bin. As he wiped his mouth with his sleeve he looked up at the statue of St. Mary majestically perched on the pediment. A great tsunami of anger swelled within him and boiled over.

"'He is the fool who hath in his heart said, There is no God'? Really?" He questioned the icon. "Well then I must be fucking barking mad!" He slowly sank back and sat down, his back to the adjoining wrought iron fence facing the cathedral. "Moves in mysterious ways is it? No mystery to me! You're either non-existent or anything but benevolent. Why the child fer fucks sake?!"

He demanded. "Why not take me, ya shit? No pleasure in that is there? Ya sadistic prick!" He kicked over the rubbish bin. "Leave the likes of me around to enjoy your handiwork, is that it?!" He extended his tantrum by standing up and kicking the tin garbage can then stomping on it until it was completely mangled.

"All knowing and all seeing? Then all know you and see this! Fuck you!" He threw two fingers at statue. "YOU BASTARD SON! I RENOUNCE YOU AND ALL YOU STAND FOR!! From this day forth, THERE IS NO GOD!" Lindsay stood, oriented himself and collected his wits. "There is no god!" He reassured himself.

Huffing and puffing he leaned into the base wall of the wrought iron fence He wiped his mouth with his handkerchief and discarded it.

Five minutes later Lindsay pushed through the front door of the Sackville Lounge, a place he had occasioned before, but only to escape the tourists swarming central Dublin in the high season.

The Stranger

On entering the Sackville Lounge for the first time one had the sensation of what it must have been like for the early Neanderthal returning home to the cave after a hard day of hunting Brontosauri and evading saber tooth tigers.

The interior of the place was eloquently appointed in Early Dark, for most drunkards, like most gamblers, preferred to engage in their chosen profession in the dark.

It was a twenty to thirty seat pub which had survived unchanged through the two hundred and fifty years since its establishment. Despite its City Centre location it had managed to maintain its ambience and character as a low budget, run down, local watering hole and so remained an island of refuge from the tourist traps infecting the area.

Save for a single, corner booth in the back a great collection of dusty, old books adorned the entire left side of the place with the bar running the entire length of the right.

Like a rat running a maze skirtin the two dozen, round, two-top tables and almost four dozen bent wood chairs was required to reach the jacks in the rear while the low ceiling would intimidate anyone prone to claustrophobia.

The utilitarian tables and chairs occupied the entire room which hadn't seen a refit since before The Great War.

The single booth, like all the tables, currently sat empty.

At just after seven that Christmas Eve it was quiet

and sparsely occupied with only two customers sitting at the far end of the bar. The middle-aged to elderly couple, (its difficult to guess age in poorly lit surroundings combined with a certain stage of alcoholism), casually glanced at the disheveled Lindsay as the stain glassed door closed over behind him.

Dressed in nineteen seventies flowered shirts and flare bottomed trousers, the two Barflies, one man one woman, looked like two over-aged extras from *Saturday Night Fever*. Lindsay shuffled to a stool at the near end of the bar by the door and plopped down.

The barflies resumed their muted conversation as the bartender worked his way down to Lindsay's end of the bar.

"Jesus John, you really look like hell! What in God's name . . .?" Lindsay nested his head between his folded arms on the bar.

"Fuck god!" He mumbled from between his arms. "Give us a double Bushmills and don't make a production of it!"

While pouring the whiskey at the back bar the bartender knitted his brow when, in the mirror he noticed a young man sitting in the corner booth. The man, impeccably groomed and dressed in a finely tailored, three piece suit, silk tie and Italian shoes smiled and nodded to the barman. He had't seen him come in but shrugged it off.

"Bloody Mary Eamon. If you please." The man, called over in a distinct American accent. Eamon brought Lindsay his whiskey then made his way back down the bar.

"Sorry, this ain't no cocktail lounge. It's a working man's pub. Besides I ain't got no tomato juice."

"I noticed a carton under the back bar last time I was in." The stranger insisted. Eamon narrowed his eyes but glanced under the back bar anyway.

"I told you I ain't got no-"

"No, further down. Directly under the till, next to the back-up Drambuie." The man instructed. The barman rummaged around and found an unopened carton of Libby's tomato juice.

Fresh squeezed for your satisfaction.

Puzzled, the barman mixed the drink and brought it over to the booth.

"How's come I never seen you in here before?" Eamon challenged.

"Must have been on your day off." He sipped his Bloody Mary. "Kudos Eamon! You really should reconsider and convert this place into a cocktail lounge!"

"Humpf!" The barman grunted and walked away.

"John you alright? You want another drink?" Eamon asked. A haggard and drained Lindsay pushed his empty glass forward.

"Fuck God!" Lindsay again mumbled as Eamon left to pour John another whiskey.

"You say something John?"

"To hell with God!" Jonathan imperceptibly mumbled.

"That's my cue!" The stranger in the booth quietly declared.

"Sorry to hear about Mary. She was a good woman." Eamon said as he served John his second glass.

"I knew your wife as well Doctor Lindsay!" Barfly Number One called down from the fra end of the bar. "She was a beautiful lady. And you know me I'm no judge of women." Barfly One sincerely offered his condolences.

"Neither was your father!" Barfly Number Two quipped as she leisurely flipped through a two year old magazine.

"Haven't you two got a home to go to? It's Christmas Eve fer fecks sake!" Eamon yelled down the bar.

"It is Christmas Eve Eamon and have ya not noticed,

we are home!"

"I'll think ta drat!" Barfly Two echoed and the two toasted their near empty pints of cider.

"Fierce sad situation with them pedophile rings on the internet." Barfly One offered.

"What'd ya expect? Global warming, El Nino and all that carry on with the Flood Tribunal? Bound to take a toll!" Barfly Two responded. "But tt Reagan fella! What a looker, hey?" She elbowed Barfly One.

Eamon approached them and, in an aggravated state, ripped the magazine from the bar.

"Laurel and Fickin' Hardy! Will you two shut yer holes! That man not only devoted 59 years in medicine to children, but left his entire fortune to Our Lady's Children's Hospital! Now fer once in yer miserable existences show a little consideration to others! Well yer at it, have pity on a man with seven kids and a wife not yet introduced to the word frugal! Order a another pint, fer fuck's sake!"

Working his way across the floor, drink in hand, the young man gleefully mumbled to no one in particular.

"Been waitin' for this for eighty-seven years!"

"What was it all for?" Jonathan moaned to himself.

"Washington D.C. here I come!" Bloody Mary in hand the young man made his way around the tables and to the far end of the bar and took the stool next to Lindsay's.

"Evening John, or do you prefer Jonathan? Both lovely names! You ever get that feeling in your stomach like the bottom of the bottomless pit was falling out?" He offered.

"Fuck off!" Lindsay snapped.

"That's the spirit man! I knew you were gonna be a challenge!"

"Give the man a bit of peace will ya!? He's had a hard way to go." Eamon chastised.

"Give us a minute." The stranger begged. "We're

old friends." He cajoled as he produced a hundred pound note and slid it across the bar to Eamon who stared in disbelief. "You know, from back during the war." The stranger added.

"You some kind'a therapist or something?" Eamon queried as the note instantly found its way into the barman's hip pocket.

"You might say that." He answered and gently nodded down towards the barflies. "And Eamon old boy, give those two a refill on me." He threw a fifty on the bar which Eamon quickly snatched up before scurrying away. "Everyone believes in something." The stranger mumbled before turning back to Lindsay.

"John."

"Aren't I after telling you to fuck off?!" He snapped then threw back his whiskey.

"I know what you're going through John. I just want you to know, I'm here to . . ." Lindsay, ignoring the stranger's pitch stood upright on the cross bars of his bar stool and called over to Eamon who was down in the center of the bar.

A low, peel of thunder sounded in the distance.

"EAMON! You still got that hurling stick back there behind the bar?" Eamon didn't respond but appeared frozen in place, the Bulmers cider he was pulling likewise hung in a state of suspended animation from the tap, into the half-filled glass. "EAMON!" Lindsay yelled again.

"He can't hear you John" Lindsay gawked over at the man, head in hand sipping his cocktail with a contemptuous look masking his face. "John, do us a favor Old Boy, have a look in the mirror." The smug stranger suggested.

"What?"

"Just look in the mirror." Lindsay made no attempt to move. "Tell you what, if you don't like what you see, I'll leave you alone. I'll go away." He sipped his drink.

Lindsay stepped down off his stool, leaned over and slowly glanced into the mirror of the side bar. Dumfounded, his jaw dropped open at the face of the man staring back at him.

It was the face of a man, himself fifty years his junior. Jonathan fell off his stool.

"You okay Old Chum?" The man dismounted his stool and helped Lindsay up off the bar room floor. "Must be more careful with that whiskey. Put you in the hospital before you know it!" Once on his feet Jonathan again stared into the mirror.

"What the fuck is this?!" Jonathan grabbed the stranger by the lapels. "What'd you do to me?"

"I didn't do anything John. You did!"

Dashing around to the front of the bar Jonathan gaped into the back bar mirror there, and as he did so he came to the realization that his 21 year old limp was now gone. He stated again at Eamon frozen at the beer taps.

Displaying an effort that would shame an Olympian Lindsay vaulted the bar and drew his face close to the glass where he ran his hand over his youthful features.

He stepped back and flexed his legs then did several quick squats in rapid succession. He turned and stared at the colorful barflies, less than a yard away. Poking them with his finger yielded no response.

"This is a trick! What is it? Some kind of eternal youth spell? You slip something in my whiskey, ya bastard?!"

"No. As of right now you still die in three years, and five months, aged ninety. Heart attack, in your sleep. No pain. Quite lucky actually."

"Why do I have the sneakin' suspicion you're manicured, sticky little fingers are here ta sell me somthin'? Somthin' I don't need, want or desire?"

"John, John, John! We've been friends two minutes, you've lost half a century off your life, the arthritis is gone from your hip and I'm trying to buy you a drink.

How can you greet that with suspicion?"

Lindsay remained behind the bar but made his way back over to the stranger.

"Who the hell are you and no cute answers!"

"An emissary John. That's all."

"Emissary? The Vatican must be in deep shit if you're all they got left!"

"Right pew John, wrong church. If it'll make things easier, you can call me Chad."

Just then the door opened and a late, middle-aged woman, plainly dressed entered the poorly lit bar room. Nodding to John and Chad she quietly made her way to a table against the left hand wall, took a book from her hand bag and began to read. Chad took notice.

"You tryin' to tell me you're . . .?!"

"What'd ya expect? Pacino? DiNero maybe?" Chad pushed up from his stool. "But in answer to your query, no I'm not The Big Guy. Just one of the minions. Excuse me."

Chad walked over to the woman who now also appeared to be under the mysterious spell, frozen in time. Chad lifted the thick novel from her hands, tore out the last page then returned the book to her hands. Walking back to his stool he touched the page with his left index finger setting it alight. Blowing the ashes through the air he then turned back to Lindsay.

"Why did you do that?"

"General mischief." He shrugged.

"How's she gonna know how it ends?!"

"Please! It's Stephanie Meyers! It ends in the first chapter!"

To the theme of *The Simpsons* a mobile phone rang. Chad opened his Armani jacket to reveal an array of half a dozen mobile phones and selected one.

"Yeah?" He took an electronic note pad from his breast pocket. "Millennium Park, London, right. Got it." He hung up. "You have a mobile phone John?"

"No. My time is my own. Jesus, all those phones must cost you a fortune!"

"Nah. We have people at Eircom, Deutche Telecom and British Telecom. But AT&T are our closest allies! They're the ones who work closest with us."

"Uh huh."

"I must tell you, for an 87 year old who drinks so heavy, you're looking pretty good."

Perhaps it was the whiskey but Jonathan seemed to be taking events in stride now. He took the bottle from the shelf and poured himself another drink.

"Care for one?"

"Thank you, no. Whiskey makes me do weird things."

"**Weird** things?! Really?"

"Yeah but only when I'm stressed."

"Huh, stressed. I didn't start drinking until I was two years from my pension. Now I only drink once a year. Not enough to get drunk, just enough to numb the pain."

"Which seems to get more intense every year, doesn't it John?" Another mobile rang to the tune of *Fair City*.

"Hallo. Look, I'm in the middle of something right now, can this wait? Alright, the Millennium Bridge. Got it. And the Millennium Dome. Very original. When I'm finished here! Check in with Dispatch and hold all my calls." Chad directed.

Lindsay did his shot and poured himself a fourth.

"Busy guy, huh?"

"Never ends! No pun intended." Chad chuckled.

"Look, just in case this is the part where you show me how I affected so many other people through the miracle of life, so I'll buy whatever it is you're sellin', save your breath. I have no intention of committing suicide."

Chad laughed. "Do I look like my name is Clarence? This is not about suicide. That would be very bad!"

"EAMON!" John shouted. "EAMON!" Lindsay yelled but there was no reaction. "Why can't he hear me?"

"I put a block on him."

"A block, how the hell did'ja manage that?"

"Simple. Greed. He choose the money over standing his ground in defense of you, his friend for over twenty years."

"There's other people in the room. The girl in the corner, with the novel?"

"Christine. She'll be 39 on Saint Valentine's Day. Her mother taught her never give up her virginity till she was married. She listened to her mother. Now it's just her, a 38 year old virgin, her chastity and a very large collection of pulp fiction novels."

John nodded over at the two barflies.

"What about those two?"

"Told them the drinks were on the house all night."

"But Eamon's been taking their money from the bar all night!"

"Never said I told Eamon. Besides he's a publican. If there's money in the room he'll claim it. I blocked these people so as long as you're in the presence of a spirit from the other realm, no mortal can see or hear you or the spirits."

"Why?"

"Had to, it's sort of a rule."

"Sounds like a dopey fuckin' rule! You yokes got a rule book with all this malarkey written down somewhere?"

"Unfortunately not. Although we've cut deals with millions of writers, none of them seems interested in writing a rule book. I've asked around. They always say it'll never get it published. Plus they're always complainin' about not bein' able to distinguish the good guys from the bad guys, or some such nonsense."

"So how do I get a drink without stealing it?"

Lindsay challenged. Chad nodded and Lindsay's glass spontaneously refilled itself. With an additional snap of the fingers, Jonathan had a double sitting on the bar in front of him." Jonathan, by this point feeling pretty good, smiled and nodded approvingly.

"You must be an angel!"

"Please, let's not cast aspersions!"

"Sorry, I forgot."

"It's okay. Why not suicide?"

"What?"

"Why not suicide, you said not suicide, why not? It's a mortal sin, if you kill yourself you wouldn't even have to wait around, you'd go straight to the front of the line! It's like getting' into every night club you ever wanted, the big burly bouncer can't stop ya, you're always on the list!" Chad proposed.

"Bollocks, it's not the mortal sin thing! I'm a stone cold coward. Could never bring myself to do it. Coming to terms with the death of a loved one is difficult enough. Facing your own mortality is even worse."

"I know exactly how you feel!" He finished off his second Bloody Mary. "But you do get straight in, saves a helluv'a lotta hassle!"

"How do you figure?" Jonathan asked.

"Like I said you'd go straight to hell, do not pass heaven do not collect two hundred dollars."

"True except for one little detail."

"What detail?"

"Suicide is one of the deadlier mortal sins, set forth at the Council of Nicea, 325 A.D. Destroys the saving grace of the soul, therefore can never be forgiven. The soul is lost, forever. You don't get it, God doesn't get it nobody gets it. One of the sins where if committed you not only go to hell, but lose your soul. Game over! And since my soul is what this little song and dance is all about. You get me but not my soul! I rest my case."

"You a doctor or a bloody lawyer?"

"Six years at the Christian Brothers Primary School, three years at the Christian Brothers Middle School and another three years at the Sisters of Charity Secondary Academy. That's twelve years of Canon Law, heavily spiced with mass six days a week, plus holidays. Law school's only four years."

"I see why they sent me to sign you up!"

"Speaking of which, of all the millions why my soul? You must have some pretty high ranking people down there at your place. Why an 87 year old doctor? I don't even go to church on a regular basis."

"You're a good Christian, why not church?"

"I've come to see church as some yoke's way of carving out a living without ever really having to do any work or get a real job."

"I see." A somewhat surprised Chad said.

"Going to church doesn't make you any more of a Christian than standing in a garage makes you a car!"

"That's good, that's very good! Mind if I use that?"

"Help yourself."

"Since you mention it, I actually do have the souls of some very prominent people. Military generals, most lawyers-"

"You mean your collection is mostly made of lawyers?"

"No, no. I mean I have most lawyers who ever lived. Shit loads of politicians, bankers-"

"In other words, the usual suspects."

"Precisely."

"Okay. So why me?" Lindsay enquired as he retrieved a second rocks glass from the end of the bar and set it in front of Chad and poured him a whiskey, making it a point to tap his glass to Chads's indicating they should toast. They did and Chad drank. Lindsay quickly poured a second and a minute later a third.

"Why you, you ask. Because my good doctor, by the last census the approximate ratio of truly 'good' people to lousy bastards is around 1.75 million to one. Oh don't get me wrong there are thousands of folks who are really good at seeming to be 'good' people, some have even refined it to an art form. But you Doctor Lindsay, you are one of those most rare of breeds who has never, not once in your life so far as we can tell, has ever acted with malice towards anyone, not once in your entire life! Hell you're even panged with guilt if you wish somebody harm, even in your deepest darkest anger, you never did anything to screw anybody over. "

"Until tonight."

"We'll, there was good reason, but let's not go there."

Having duped Chad with an old school Irishman's trick by throwing back a half dozen drinks and acting a bit uncoordinated in the hopes of appearing drunker than he actually was, Lindsay decided to make his move.

Reaching under the bar he produced a bottle of Poitin he knew Eamon kept there and poured Chad and himself a healthy measure leaving the bottle on the bar.

"What's this?"

"Poitin, Irish moonshine. Ever had it before?"

"Had it? Never heard of it."

"Made from potatoes. Try it."

"Hmm, I like potatoes." Chad beamed as he took the glass and sniffed it. "Looks like water."

"In a way it is." Lindsay explained. Chad decided it was harmless enough and threw back the glass in time to hear Jonathan explain.

"We call it Holy Water."

Chad nearly choked and jumped off the stool as he tried to spit out what was left of the drink in his mouth.

"Relax! It's just a saying! It's just moonshine!" Jonathan teased as he refilled their glasses.

"Truly sorry for what you're going through John. I truly am." Chad appeared to sympathize as he wobbled a bit climbing back up onto his stool.

"Thanks for your understanding, but my wife's been dead for what seems an eternity now. How about we cut the bullshit and get to the point?"

"Very impressive my good Doctor. Way to bounce back from adversity!" Chad, genuinely impressed, smirked as his Bloody Mary glass spontaneously refilled itself.

"Where were you when I was skint?" Lindsay quipped as he stared at Chad's now full glass. John poured two more shots

"Ohhhh . . . I was around. Are you interested?"

Lindsay, using his glass nudged Chad's measure of Poitin closer to him and held his own up to toast. Chad obliged.

"AGGHHH! You sure that's only potatoes?"

"Make a man outta ya, hey?" Lindsay badgered. "You were saying?"

"I was about to ask what would you say if I told you I can guarantee that you would always look like you do right now? Thirty-five years old, never get sick and never be diseased?"

"What?"

"My proposition. I'm propositioning you John!" Chad giggled at his sophmorphic joke.

"Stay young forever, never grow old? Can't see much wrong with that." Jonathan said. Chad smiled. "Except as soon as someone noticed I'd have to pack up and relocate. Then there's the fact that I'd have to give up medicine, find a new profession, could never fall in love, remarry or have any long lasting, meaningful relationships. Can't see much gain in that."

Chad wobbled as he sat back and stared at John.

"No. That'd be my answer to that little proposition. No." Lindsay reiterated.

"Just 'no'?!"

"Okay, hell no. Or do you guys say, 'Heaven no!'"

"Oh come on John, don't tell me you haven't

thought about it?"

"Oh I won't lie. I've thought about it, everybody has."

"Well than, what would it take?"

"I doubt there's anything you could-"

"What would you say if I proposed that it is possible to guarantee that no more children would ever again die on Christmas Eve?"

"Now you're a messenger from God?"

"Now you're getting belligerent!"

"No kids dying on Christmas Eve! Piss off!"

"Do I sense doubt?"

"Doubt? How 'bout this? You're a fuckin' nutter! Now piss off!" Lindsay lifted his glass but before it reached his lips the poitin in it had vanished. "Now that's just mean!" Lindsay declared.

Lindsay's head involuntarily jerked around as, outside in the street, he heard a child's giggling emanate through the pub door. He dashed to the window in time to see the little girl in the red beret and wool coat, and her mum loaded with packages, walking by the pub.

Suppressing his joy he quickly transitioned to disbelief then suspicion as he slowly walked back to Chad.

"How 'bout that, Doctor Jonathan Michael Lindsay? Have I got your attention now?"

"How'd you do that?! Hypnosis? It ain't real! Can you bring anybody back?!"

"Afraid not old boy. You see she was a, how would you say it? A bit of –"

"A fuck up?! Is that it? You fucked up somewhere and she wasn't supposed to-"

"Wasn't supposed to be taken, exactly. Even in the other realm accidents happen. That's why I'm offering you this deal. It's one way to avoid any future accidents." Chad then leaned in, took Lindsay by the lapel and whispered in confidence, "Plus, I'm not that crazy about going in front of the Big Guy and not having a solution to this ah . . . mess."

"And the payoff is?"

"How do you mean?"

"Oh, I just fell off the cabbage truck this morning! What's in it for you?" Lindsay demanded.

"All I want is what anybody wants. Any hard working young man deserves! I want to move up."

"Move up? You want **me** to help get **you** a promotion?"

"Yeah a promotion. Why not?"

"What kind'a promotion?"

"Now we're talkin'! You'll be visited by two more spirits who will . . ."

Lindsay looked at Chad with a wry eye and balked in disbelief.

"I know, I know! It's been done. What can I tell you? I don't make the rules."

"I thought there was supposed to be three spirits?"

"We're downsizing. The spirits will tell you a little more about our world, what you can expect and why you should sign with us." Chad pushed up off his stool and, still slightly wobbly, made his way towards the door. "Did I mention you get to live forever?" Chad added as he headed pushed through the door.

"Live forever?! What the hell for? So I have no incentive to get out of bed in the morning? Live forever. So I can watch everyone I have ever or will ever fall in love with skowly rot and die before me?!"

"You're a strange duck Lindsay, you know that?" Chad made a duck sound and laughed to himself as he pushed through the door.

"Live forever?! That a promise or a threat?" Glancing down he saw that his glass was again full. He threw back the drink.

Eamon stopped pulling the two ciders, served them to the barflies and went down to Lindsay.

"You say something John?" He nodded down at the doctor's empty glass. "Sorry mate, didn't notice you were dry."

"You can hear me?" An astounded Lindsay asked.

"Of course I can hear you! You think I went deaf all of a sudden?" He spied the bottle of poitin on the bar. "Hey! What the hell you doing with my poitin?!"

"You gave it to me! Don't you remember?"

"Oh. Sorry John." He poured Lindsay a small measure and restowed the bottle back underneath the bar.

The Messengers

Jonathan, beginning to sober up by now, was unsure of the events he has just experienced. Glancing around the room he saw the four other people in the bar apparently oblivious to any abnormalities. Reluctantly and with great apprehension he again rose up on his bar stool to look into the mirror. The younger version of himself stared back. He looked at his glass of poitin and drank it.

"Eamon!"

"What?"

"Eamon, come down here will ya?!" The barman served the two pints to the Barflies then made his way back down to Lindsay's end of the bar.

"What is it John?"

"How's my color lookin' to you Eamon?" He brandished his face at various angles to give Eamon a good look.

"Fine. Better actually. Much better colour. Why you feelin' okay are ya?"

"Ahh . . . yeah, yeah I am."

"Uisce beatha!" Eamon declared referring to the poitin. "Do it every time!"

"Yeah. The water of life. Thanks Eamon!" Lindsay fell back onto his stool. "Must be it. Must'a been the moonshine." He told himself.

Just then the toilet door in the back of the place swung open and two figures emerged.

The man, tall and muscular, was a stereotypical, well-built Aryan. Dressed in tan, neatly pressed slacks, grey trainers and a white tee shirt which bore a portrait of Freud, he patiently listened with feigned attentiveness as the female with him finished relating a joke.

She continually sliced the air with an oversized French cigarette nestled into an obnoxiously long, black and gold holder and was clothed in a tight black leather corset and form fitting pants. Her stiletto heels clacked across the bar room floor. The shapely blond employed animated gesticulations to relay the end of her story. Without acknowledging him they moved to Lindsay's end of the bar.

She spoke with a heavy French accent.

". . . and everyone is standing around up to their knees in shit, smoking cigarettes, and telling stories. So the politician says, 'This isn't so bad! I'll spend the rest of eternity in this room.' The devil leaves and locks the door behind him. A few minutes later another devil enters and says, 'Okay, smoke break's is over! Everybody back on your heads!'"

She laughed hysterically at her own joke. Her companion, then replied in a thick German accent.

"I find your story, although exaggerated, amusing. However, it is a well-established fact that humor is the opiate of the id."

"Meard Brad! Get ze rod out of your ass!" The woman leaned into Lindsay. "Germans! No sense of humour!" She confided.

"Dr. John Lindsay?" The Aryan inquired.

"Yes." He looked round the bar room and realized that Eamon and the others were again frozen in mid action. "Shit! Here we go again!"

"We are so pleased to make your acquaintance. I am Brad, and zis is. . ."

She stroked Lindsay's cheek. "He is so smooth! I will call him Johnny!" She declared. "I am Tad, your dream girl, Cheri." Her hand slid to his thigh. "Brad can zis not wait? I'm sure zere's a back room here somewhere." She cajoled.

"Will you control yourself for once! Sheisse

Französische!"

"Control is for mortals, Dahling!"

"We have been sent here to clarify for you what is being offered."

"I've got a pretty good idea what's being offered." He gently lifted Tad's hand from his leg. "But tell me, why would I want to trade this world for yours?" Lindsay casually inquired.

"Because in your world Herr Doctor, everything is wrong way around." Brad argued.

"Everything that's fun is a sin. . ." Tad clarified.

"Or, even more amusingly, illegal."

"Sex, drugs. . ."

"Rock and roll!"

"Rock and roll's not illegal!" Lindsay protested.

"Really?! Based on the music we've been hearing lately, we assumed it was."

"Some of these young people have pretty good music." Jonathan defended.

"Such as?" Brad asked.

"Such as Lady RaRa." Tad sarcastically interjected.

"Don't you get it?!" Brad explained. "That's why we gave you boy bands and female pop stars! As punishment for killing rock and roll!"

"Also there is always arguing about who's in charge, men or women." She took a long drag on her perpetually smoldering cigarette. "Neither! You're always too busy fighting each other." Argued Tad.

"The sexual rivalry concept of yours was a stroke of genius!"

"Easy as Ying and Yang!"

"Oh quit your bragging! Think how far humans could have progressed by now if it weren't for their sexual cold war?" Brad added.

"And the best thing about it is, they explain it away with insipid clichés like 'Men are from Mars, women are from Venus!"

"And the race thing, you've got it all wrong. Whites call blacks, Hispanics and Orientals minorities! Whites are less than 1% of the entire earth! In reality, you are za minorities!"

"It's meant as a guide line for equality in society! To foster respect amongst people." Lindsay argued.

"That's exactly it, you're people. You're incapable of respecting one another!"

"Did'ja ever think you'd live to see the day you'd have to speak Chinese to get a hamburger on O'Connell Street?"

"Wouldn't you love to leave all that behind? Join the privileged few on the inside? Those of us who are in the know?" Tad coaxed.

"Yeah, looks like you're having a real ball!"

"C'mon! It'll be fun! You think Oppenheimer just happened to get inspiration to invent the atomic bomb?"

"Why do you suppose it took Salk so long to find the vaccine for poliomyelitis?"

"We kept switching the serum! We do good things too, Johnny."

"We're not asking you to do any field work for us." Brad explained.

"Close deals on clients, things like zat."

Lindsay sat back against the bar and smiled.

"Youse two sound like a couple of lawyers to me."

"Aw John! We're not zat bad are we? Com'on, what do you say?"

"I tell lads, as miserable as I am here, fire and brimstone sound even less appealing. I'll give it a pass." Lindsay said.

"I think you misunderstand what's on offer here John. It's not like that." Brad explained. "All that fire and brimstone nonsense was dreamt up by John Calvin!"

"Scots! Always find the more miserable side of everything!"

"But we did like the idea."

"That's why we saved a special place for him!"

"You mean John Calvin is?

"Of course!"

"You suppose they knew anything about cholinesterase, acetylcholine and transfer across the neural synaptic junctions and the resulting hallucinatory effects back in the thirteenth century?

"Congratulations on your neurochemistry Tad, but what the hell are you on about?" Lindsay challenged.

"Some paranoid delusional Italian eats –"

"A writer no less." Tad added.

"Eats some bad rye, falls asleep on a hillside, dreams about all these rooms and levels of hell, wakes up and tells everybody about some ridiculous sign at the gates and right away the underworld gets a bad rap for the rest of eternity!"

"'Abandon Hope All Ye Who Enter Here!'" She recited with an ominous voice. "PLEASE! You think the Church didn't jump on that fantasy like the Irish Film Board on an American backed film script?"

"John, ve believe each man has his personal version of hell. I'd say yours is watching children die every day. Why would you not want to leave zat behind?"

Lindsay threw back his shot started to call out to Eamon for a refill but then realizded it was pointless. Brad smiled pointed at John's glass. It refilled itself.

"Huh!" Lindsay grunted. "It occurs to me that you guys must want the likes of me something fierce. It further occurs to me that anyone dyeing anywhere in or around Christmas is just as devastating as kicking it on Christmas. So, tell what I'm prepared to do." Tad stopped waving her cigarette about and the both leaned in to listen. "I'll seriously consider your offer n one condition." The two messengers perked up. "For no one dying December twenty-third to January second." Lindsay said.

"John! That's totally unreasonable!"

"You cannot be serious"

"That's my offer."

"A wheeler dealer! I'm impressed!" Tad commented.

"We're authorized children only, and that only for one night!"

"I always say a hard man is good to find!" Tad giggled as her hand slipped back onto Lindsay's thigh which he quickly removed. He turned back towards his drink.

"Send Chad back here. I'll discuss it with him." Jonathan quietly insisted, snuffing them off.

They attempted several more times to renegotiate but were meant with total disregard for their presence.

Finally Tad and Brad exchanged glances, and resigned themselves to their failure, and exited through the side door, arguing. (ELAB!)

"So much for the B side." Jonathan quipped as he noticed the room recede to normal.

"Eamon!" He called.

The Negotiation

Checking his watch Lindsay saw that it had been less than ten minutes since he wandered into the *Sackville* and took a seat at the bar. He then noticed that the sweep hand on his watch suddenly stopped. He looked up to see Chad entering.

As he entered through the front door, Chad was plagued by yet another phone call. He answered it.

"What?! I asked you to hold my calls! The Millennium Wheel, alright got it! When I'm finished here!" He hung up and took the bar stool next to Lindsay.

"Trouble at the office, dear?" Lindsay jibbed. He noticed the four others in the room were again frozen in place. He slid off his chair, reached back under the bar and retrieved the poitin.

"That was my detailer. I've got some errands to run over in England."

"Tell me about this promotion." Jonathan cajoled as he poured himself and Chad a drink.

"Like I said, all I want is what anybody wants. Deserves!" He took his drink. "I want to move up. I've been working third world countries for three and a half long years." Chad mood had noticeably changed.

"Most of your adult life huh?"

"Very funny!"

"Have a another drink. You look-" Chad cut him off as he leaned in to speak.

"Can I . . . can I let you in on something? I mean something personal. I don't get to confide in anyone much." He downed his drink. Lindsay quickly poured another.

"Love to hear it."

"Confidentially, my track record hasn't really been what it should be lately. Two years ago I was assigned to Sinead O'Connor."

"And?"

"I'm supposed to get her manager to book this huge concert in Rome, and on stage she's gonna renounce God. What happens? She takes the fucking vows! Becomes a priest! ON STAGE! It's like getting to shag Miss World, next thing ya find out, the night before she turns lesbian!"

"Tough one." Lindsay said.

"Next they send me to the BBC to get *Coronation Street-*"

"The sappy, shitty soap opera?"

"Yeah. Get it extended indefinitely. That didn't work out. Next I'm supposed to get Michael Jackson busted on another kiddie porn rap."

"That shouldn't been too hard. What happened?"

"WHAT HAPPENED? What happened is he opens a multimillion dollar kids charity and people are tripping over themselves to give him money and get involved! He's a hero!"

"Things just not flowing your way, huh?"

"Next thing I hear, he's over dosed by his greed ridden doctor! The L.A. D.A. blows the trial, just like with O.J., Jackson's not exposed, he since O.D's again, it's an accidental death and he winds up in purgatory forever! We don't get him, the other guy doesn't get him! I'm telling ya Lindsay, there is no justice!"

"Have a drink!"

"You've no idea!"

"Best laid plans, huh?" Lindsay refilled their glasses. "So tell me, where's this promotion to?"

"Nowhere if I don't pull this off!"

"I see."

"It's more like a lateral move actually, an

assignment we all dream of."

"Really?"

"Yeah! It's a place where it's virtually impossible not to be a success! Impossible to screw up."

"Washington D.C.?" He poured Chad another drink. "So quite a lot riding on this deal, huh?"

"If I don't pull this off it's good-bye white collar work and back to the blue collar division!"

"Blue collar division?"

"Tempting bored, middle-aged housewives to cheat on their husbands with bored middle aged losers!"

"You really want this Washington gig, huh?"

"You kiddin'?! It's every minion's dream to work in the American capital! There or London. Problem is they don't need that many of us in London. In D.C. people line up to sign deals. You got'a love a town that's in a country of 350 million people who believe they elect their own leaders."

"Uh huh. Well, you now my terms. You really want D.C. you know what you got'a do."

Staring eye-to-eye they touched glasses and threw back their shots.

From his inner breast pocket Chad produced a one page contract and laid it out on the bar.

"A single page?" Jonathan was shocked.

"Yeah, no lawyers so there's no fine print. You'd be surprised at how much simpler life is without lawyers."

"No I wouldn't."

"No need to read it! Boiler plate stuff, Just sign here, here, initial here and sign and initial here and here."

Ignoring the document Lindsay poured Chad another, slightly larger drink of Poitin.

"How do I know you won't renege on your end of it?" Lindsay challenged.

"Thank you, thank you! People always confuse us with Santa Claus. They think we have this big book with everybody's name in it and we put X's and O's by their names. That's not it at all."

"Go on." Lindsay encouraged.

"99% of our clientele are referrals. Friends recommending friends, you know as a final joke. Employees suggesting their bosses. Husbands recommending ex-wives. We get a lot of those."

"I'm beginning to see the connection."

"Exactly! Do you have any idea how much of a pain in the ass it would be if we got a reputation for not keeping our word? That's another reason we don't use lawyers to make up these contracts." Chad, now feeling very relaxed, threw back his drink. "Oh Yahweh! That stuff's terrific!!"

"You alright?" John asked.

Chad suddenly reached into his Armani suit jacket and produced a red phone and dialed.

"Just got a brain-storm." He whispered over to Jonathan. "Hello Central? Give me the Main Detailer! Adolf? Listen to this! You are gonna fall of your seat when you here this one! We invent a virus, a computer virus. We call it, a bug, the Millennium virus. No! 'The Millennium Bug'! Yeah that's it, 'The Millennium Bug'! Then we start the rumor that it's gonna wipe out all the computers on the planet at midnight on New Year's! Yeah, New Year's! Great idea or what?! What'a ya mean people'd never be that stupid? What about eight track tapes?! Yeah, exactly! So, what about it? Yeah but, Adolf, if they don't buy it it'll scare hell outta them till New Years! Oh yeah?! Same to you!" In disgust Chad hung up. "Fuckin' bureaucrats!"

"No joy?"

"Prick! Probably implement it and take credit for himself. So much for the incentive program, huh? Where were we?"

"Ya know Chad, I've taken a funny kind of liking to you these last few . . . few whatevers." John poured two more shots, nearly the last of the bottle and raised his glass.

"Cheers John!" Chad, smelling victory did likewise.

"Shlàinte Chad!" They threw back their shots and Chad was only able to stay on his bar stool with a little help from Lindsay's hand on his shoulder. Jonathan immediately returned to his argument. "Look Chad, I wanna help you out, I really do but what the hell good is it if some kid's parents die on Christmas? You don't think that's not gonna fuck up his holiday? Sorry Chad but I got'a insist, the deal is everybody! Christmas to New Years!"

"That's not the deal I was authorized to offer John! Lawyers take an oath, we can't lie!" They simultaneously burst out laughing at the joke. "Come on John, join the club! What have you got to lose? You're past you're sell by date anyway. Drippin' oil as they say in Cork. You buried your wife of fifty-odd years, on the eve of your anniversary no less. You still live in a two room flat and you drive a bicycle because you're too old to drive now days fer cryin' out loud!"

"So?"

"SO!? After all you've given to this community! After all that money and free service you gave to the Children's Hospital? You think they'd at least name a wing after you! A hallway, a toilet-"

"A broom closet!" Lindsay joked.

"Something! All those years helping kids. Helping them, holding their hands as life ebbed from their tiny bodies and did that bastard up stairs ever let you and your wife have your own?"

"Mary. . . she. . ." Chad sensed Lindsay weakening.

"I know. John, you've played by the rules your whole life. Poverty, chastity and obedience. You're a god-damned monk in all but the way you dress fer cryin' out loud! You've been faithful as a sheep dog to that absentee landlord up there your entire life. What's it got ya?" He paused to let it sink in. "Well?"

The poitin nearly gone, Chad poured them both one last drink.

"So you can't renege?" Lindsay reaffirmed.

"Not a chance."

"And if someone dies?"

"Trust me. No one's going to die."

"If someone does die?!"

"You're off the hook and I'm screwed! It's bored housewives for me, forever. In exchange we can't take anyone for the interim period agreed, for . . . eternity."

"And my end?"

"Your soul belongs to us."

"I know that part. I mean what about not taking anybody during Christmas?"

"Not anybody. No kids."

"What the hell good is that? Everybody! Christmas to New Year's or no deal'

"John! That's not the deal I was auth-"

"You want to see Washington? Think of the possibilities Chad old boy! New administration coming in. All those young ones wanting to get ahead of the big game, all those juicy scandals yet to come. A bright go-getter like yerself. If you tried hard enough, I'll bet you might even get them to break Clinton's record! Maybe even Nixon's, who knows?!"

"NIXON's record! OH MAN, wouldn't that be somethin'!" Chad daydreamed of the possibilities. Then snapped out of it. "John you're being unreasonable!"

"Use the red phone. Everybody lives or we'll see what happens in a few years." Lindsay points up to the sky.

"Oh alright! What the heaven, it's Xmas. Not my best day anyway. New Year's, now there's a holiday! All that drinking and driving! Drug abuse! Arguments! I get giggly just thinking about it! It used to be a lot better till some prick came up with the seat belt. Then that breathalyzer gizmo set us back quite a bit. Thank Satan

105

for the Eighties and designer drugs!"

Chad quickly scribbled out a clause on the bottom of the contract. Lindsay noticed the heading on the paper.

"Office of the Attorney General of the United States stationary?" He read aloud.

"Yeah we get it free. Professional courtesy. Loads of connections there." As he writes Chad notices Lindsay dips his finger in the alcohol and produces a pocket knife. "What are you doin'?"

"Making ready to sign the contract!"

"In blood? John, last time you went to the movies did you sit next to the organist? We don't do that anymore! Besides, it's sooo unhygienic! And you're a doctor!"

Producing a small box device, Chad takes Lindsay's thumb and places it inside one of the two openings on top. Chad follows suit. "DNA scanner. Got it from the Los Angeles D.A.'s office. They were giving them away after the O.J. thing." A low hum followed by a ticking sound emanated from the device. Seconds later the ping of a microwave bell sounded and Chad removed the device from Lindsay's finger and pocketed it.

Giddy with a combination of his coup and the moonshine, Chad giggled to himself.

"Sort'a like Star Trek, huh? Ever wondered what Scotty was doin' down there in the engine room? Maybe he had the make-up girl bent over a console." He elbowed Lindsay as he hopped down off his seat and assumed a bad Scottish accent while he began miming sex with a woman as he pretend humped his bar stool. "I'm given 'er all I've got Captain! I'm a man not a machine! She's gettin' ready ta blow!" Only he laughed at his own joke. Lindsay stared at him as if he were cracking up. "Scottie. Star Trek. Captain Kirk? Never mind."

"Is that it then? Nothing else?"

"Just one more thing, a question." Chad enquired.

"Yeah?"

"What the fuck is a yoke?"

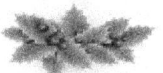

Lindsay Strikes

The Sackville Lounge
24 December, 1988

The Barflies occupied their usual place watching Eamon who wrestled with changing a keg. The middle-aged spinster occupied the same table, however now she was sharing a drink with a male companion.

Gaily whistling a tune, Chad entered the bar.

"How'r'ya! You're Chad, ain't ya?" Eamon recognized him.

"At your service my good Eamon! May I have one of your delicious Bloody Mary's please?"

"Yeah, no problem. John Lindsay left this for ya." Eamon tossed an envelope across the bar to Chad before starting to mix Chad's cocktail. "Says to say, 'Happy Christmas'."

"Thank you Eamon." Taking a seat at the bar, Chad opened it.

Instantly his face became contorted with pain and disbelief as he read it.

"NOOOOO!!" He looked at his watch. It was thirty seconds to midnight.

Bursting through the front door out onto Cathedral Street he raced out to O'Connell Street and was just in time to hear the blast of a bus horn shatter the night followed by the screeching of tires and a terrible thud. Somewhere a woman screamed.

Howling like a wounded animal Chad fell to his knees.

"Oh what a world, what a world! All my beautiful work!"

Chad screamed again and vanished in a puff of smoke, his pathetic cries heard fading into the night.

Over on O'Connell Street, in front of Clery's Department Store a little girl in a red hat tugged at her mother's arm.

"Mommy, mommy! That old man was hit by a bus! Is gonna be alright?"

The End

LUCK & FAME ARE FOUR LETTER WORDS!

This work is dedicated to

Kate Kennedy

There's only one.
(Thank God)

It's common knowledge that people are the heart of any good newspaper story. The drama, the excitement. The humanity! And there are some who feel that newspapers are the heart of society. Heck, the world. Some like J.J. Hobson fer instance.

Guess I better introduce myself so you folks don't go gettin' suspicious and wonderin' why a sanitation engineer is tellin' ya'll this little story. I was hired on here as a janitor 'bout ten years ago but was promoted to Sanitation Engineer last March. It don't pay much more but Mrs. Reeves in Human Resources said folks would respect me more. They don't.

Not like my uncle Rusty, Rusty Fender. He's a English Teacher at the university in Birmingham. He's real good with words. Some folks call him a cunning linguist. Not sure why people laugh when I tell them that. They do.

My name's Eugene Amos Corn, from Alabama and I been keeping this here notebook ever since I came ta the big city ten years ago casin' I ever wanna go back to Tuscaloosa and open my own big magazine.

J.J. is the owner and man in charge with controlling interest in Rank Publishing, Ltd. The 'Ltd' ain't really an American thing but J.J. figured it sounded more sophisticated then 'Co.' and would corral the educated crowd.

This magnificent edifice of man located at 1016 Broadway, right here in the heart of the Big Apple is the J.J. Hobson Building. (That's New York City to you country folk!)

I know what you're probably thinking; What kind'a egotistical, maniacal, maniac goes and gets a 57 story building named after himself? Well, it was a smart man that's who! A smart man like J.J. Hobson.

Heck, it was J.J. himself what got them fine, college

educated architects together to draw up all them detailed plans. Then hired all them skilled builders with their welders and masons and highly trained carpenters after he went and borrowed all that money from them banks and then employed all them genius accountants to manage all that cash, pay all them highly trained manager people and then got them there lawyer folks with years and years of university to put the deal together. And he got them to do it all with other people's money!

And the best part is, if'n the business fails, J.J. don't lose a penny! Now that's smart business. OPM! That's the American Way!

Men like J.J. could see the future even before it happened and the future was newspapers, newspapers and magazines! In short, print is the wave of the future. Radio is dead. Forget T.V., he'd preach. Electronics is over rated and had absolutely no future in it. Just something the Yankees dreamed up to win the war against them Nazi fellas twenty years ago. A passing fad, nothing more.

J.J. set up the company just after the war and The Rank company publishes mainly magazines but we have one of the biggest newspapers in these here United States.

Forget pubs like *The L.A. Times*, *The Chicago Sun* or the *San Francisco Examiner*. All rags in comparison. There's only one *New York Time*!

The original name was supposed to be *The New York Times* but apparently when J.J. come up from Arkansas the name was already taken.

Our story begins up on the 47th Floor, in office #4707, row E, desk number 52A, the Literary Review desk.

At this desk sits a pretty, slight little girl, with long auburn hair of about twenty-five years old. I don't mean she's slightly a girl, or slightly like a girl! I just mean

116

she's a bit thin, which worries her father sometimes because it makes her seem a little fragile. Daddy's always think their little girls are fragile.

'Course it don't worry her mom none. She's slight too. So slight in fact that her father took her mom to a Halloween dress up party one time and when folks asked what she was supposed to be, her father would get her to stand sideways and stick out her tongue.

"She's a zipper! Get it?!" Her mom didn't laugh but folks would. Of course they didn't laugh so much the next year when her dad went naked wearin' nuthin' but a pair of roller skates.

Said he was a pull toy.

They didn't get to many more invites after that.

ʒ

Reminiscent of a thousand chickens all pecking in syncopated unison the din of dozens of typewriters dominated the expansive room whose back office seemed to be indiscernibly hidden somewhere along the back wall.

The office was once visited by Woody Allen for an interview. He stepped off the elevators and just stood there. The receptionist asked if he was alright.

"Yes. Just wondering what time the next bus stops here." He answered.

This morning at desk number 52A in Row E of office #4707 Kate advanced the carriage roller on her Underwood-Olivetti and perused the story which was due fifteen minutes ago.

No typos, as usual.

No spelling errors as usual and no grammatical faux pas, as usual.

"He'll hate it. As usual." She mumbled.

She pushed away from her desk and dutifully trod up the long aisle towards the slaughtering room of the abattoir. To the gas chamber at Leavenworth, to the ovens at Auschwitz. To the office of Harry S. Steinkopf, Editor-in-Chief of the New York Time Magazine Group.

The young attractive secretary, a temp sent over by the agency because Mrs. Dumbarton was out sick that day, sat at the desk outside his office nervously typing away as Kate approached. A quick glance to the side of the oak desk revealed the small, wire waste basket nearly half full of damp Kleenex. Further evidence of recently struck tragedy was revealed by the young blonde's slightly smeared make-up. Kate pointed at the door and the secretary sniffled a nod.

Fucking temps ought to get hazardous duty pay when they're sent over here! Kate mused.

Kennedy's knock on the door elicited a Neanderthal-like grunt. In her year at the publishing house she had become fluent in Steinkopf-ese and knew to interpret the grunt as 'enter' in human language.

Steinkopf sat behind his desk, a giant red marker in his fist bleeding all over another first draft of someone else's story.

Kate, as did most of the staff, reckoned that Steinkopf was a frustrated high school English teacher in another life. But because he psychologically scared so many enthusiastic young minds, forever stunting their academic growth, to balance the Ying and Yang of spiritual karma and restore the natural order of the universe he was reincarnated to torture those most educated of know-it-all egotists, writers.

She also did not need to consult her Steinkopf-to-English pocket dictionary to understand "Ah huh." So she took a seat in front of his Brobdingnagian desk, in the seat which had purposely had its original plush seat cushion replaced with a one inch soft foam pad in order to enable the unfortunate victim of the hot seat to sit six inches lower than the Master Inquisitor Himself.

Eyes still glued to the mutilated story in front of him

Steinkopf's left hand shot out like the oversized limb of a midget Nazi saluting Hitler as he passed on parade. Kate passed him her pages and, in one smooth motion the exsanguinated, sheets in front him were thrust into the D.O.A. basket on the right side of his desk and replaced by new meat.

In her seat she did rock while the tick tock of the large black clock in her head did knock as it grew louder.

And still he read.

Still she waited.

Finally, without a single crimson stain on a single sheet he sighed a single sigh and sat straight up in his seat.

"Kennedy, do you realize that in less than a decade people are going to walk on the moon! The Moon! I don't believe it but there's 20,000 folks down at NASA who are punchin' the overtime clock to make it happen!" Papers in hand he slowly stood to emphasize his grandiose significance. "Just last week like something out'a Frankenstein movie some crazy doctor in South Africa gave some other crazy guy a new heart!" He stared off, out the window in deep contemplation. "I wonder will that guy experience different emotions now?"

I wonder if you'd be eligible for a new heart? A used heart! Any heart!! A heart!!! Kate wondered as she feigned a smile and pretended to pay attention to Steinkopf.

"Harry, what the hell's this got to do with my story?" She finally prodded, knowing full well that Steinkopf disapproved of women who used profanity. Which is exactly why she used profanity.

"Kennedy, I'm taking the long way around the barn here tryin' to explain to you it's nineteen hundred and sixty-one and you're still shovelin' the same old stuff!" He tossed her story back on the desk. "Nobody reads the newspapers to be infiltrated with righteous indignation!

We know there's no justice in the world, that's what makes it go around! That's what drives people to become financially stable, so they can afford good lawyers and spend their free time on escapism! Why do you think God made the picture shows?"

Probably the same reason man made God! She quietly speculated.

"How in the name of Sam Hill are you gonna write that book you been batting around for the last year and a half if you-"

"I'm not writing any book!" She protested.

The reality of the situation was that Kate had never considered writing a novel. Attempting to tackle something that she was never likely to finish was pointless. The rumor that she was writing a book sprang up the day she and her last flame broke up. He had the bad manners, a strong point with Roger, to fire up an argument one day when he dropped her off at work. In the process of yelling good-bye he tagged the rip-snorting, all-night-long Donnybrook they'd been having with, "You're just like all the rest of the so-called journalists in this town! You'll never even write a book!" This comment was overheard by some of the office gossip brigade including the Queen Bee herself, Doris Huntsinger and so . . .

Kate saw it as the most cliché of all clichés, for a journalist to attempt to write a novel. A book that would actually mean something. Make a difference. It was like every architect she had ever met who thought they could design furniture or every movie star she'd read about who thought they should have a restaurant or sing in a band. *Why the hell would I labor for a year or more to set myself up for the big fall?!* She reasoned. That's easy enough to do with relationships! She logically concluded.

Kate's heart lay in the 'mission' of journalists to keep the ". . .crooked as five miles of bad mountain road" politicians and city officials in line by scrutinizing them at every turn and exposing them through the power of print. However, already three years out of university and not sure what to do with herself, Kate was learning the difference between the classroom and the press room.

Like the chase scene in a Steve McQueen police movie Steinkopf's voice once again crashed through her thoughts.

"Damn it Kennedy, we've talked about this before! You remind me of my son! I was bound and determined to teach that boy the ways of the world and even though he resisted every step of the way I was able to teach him everything that I know, and he was none the wiser!"

"So what do you want me write about Harry? About the fact that New York charities lead the nation in donations again this year?"

"I don't care! But nobody cares if JFK is making a mistake by sending advisors to Viet Nam! Heck, I'll bet you dollars to donuts you couldn't find ten people in America who knew where the heck Viet Nam is! Besides, the guys he's sending are just advisors fer cryin' out loud! What's the worst that could happen?!"

"Viet Nam is on the South China Sea in Southeast Asia, on the Laotian-Cambodian border and is under threat of invasion by the Red Chinese who back the North Vietnamese regime allied to the Communist Viet Cong. Exports include tea, rice and some silk." She countered.

"Very good! Now go find me two more people who know that and we can form a Jeopardy team! And well you're at it, find me a story that people will enjoy over their morning eggs and coffee. Not this bleeding hearts bologna that sends them off to work all hyped up!"

Snatching her story from his hand Kate made her way to the door.

Well, at least he didn't hate it. He only despised it.

It was as she was closing the office door behind her

and the temp was ripping into a new box of Kleenex that Mortimer Needlebaum, the company mail boy, looked up as he threw the bundle of mail he was holding on Betsy's Knaplock's desk ignoring the fact that half of it slid to the floor. Ignoring the spillage he hurriedly navigated his mail cart on an intercepting azimuth to cut Kate off at the pass. It was at the intersection of Rows D and E in front of desk #26 that he awkwardly feigned the encounter by accidentally on purpose cutting her off.

"Oh, hi Kate!"

"Hi Mortimer."

"Hope today is your lucky day!"

"Sometimes there's bad luck and sometimes there's good luck. But sometimes, life just sucks."

"I'm sure your luck will change!"

"Sorry Mortimer but someone stole the 'L' from my luck and replaced it with an 'F'!"

"Oh! Old Stone Head shoot you down again?!"

"Again? Yet! I just don't know what the heck he wants from me!"

"Well people can't always say what they mean. Or want, I mean. Say what they want is what I mean to say." Kate's puzzled look signaled her confusion. "What I mean is, don't get so discouraged about your writing! Lots of great writers struggled before they were great! Take Jack London fer instance!"

"Jack London was a great writer who ultimately committed suicide."

"What about Ernest Hemingway?"

"Bullet to the head just before his sixty-first birthday."

"Oh, okay sorry. How about a famous woman writer?! Virginia Woolf?!"

"Famous suicide letter to her husband. Filled her pockets with stones and walked into the river and drowned herself."

"Oh okay, what about Sylvia Plath . . . never mind."

122

"Mortimer wanna do me a big favor?"

"Sure Kate, name it!"

"I know you mean well but please, stop trying to cheer me up. Thank you."

Even Needlebaum's armor plated skull knew a direct hit when it took one and so he vanished into the background scenery of the massive office.

Shuffling back to her desk, Kate plopped down into her seat and looked about her at the bustling office.

Reporters were reporting, typists were typing and messengers were messaging, all while secretaries scurried about doing secretarial stuff.

ζ

Now here some'a ya'll might say that even though Kate was having a bad day at least the offices of Rank Publishing were bustling. But if you was to take the time to look closer, it would become obvious to you that no actual work was being done. It wasn't that everyone was lazy or dodging their work, no sirree! These was pretty honest folks, for New York Yankees I mean. Truth was everyone was trying **to look** busy on account'a **there was no work**!

Problem was even though the aconomy was doin' good, 'cause that Marshal Plan fella give all the Krauts and Japs . . . I mean Germans and Japanese, I forgot we ain't supposed ta say Krauts and Japs no more! Give them all that work making T.V.'s and radios and such, and everybody was happy, what with that young Catholic fella Kennedy getting' elected and all, there was still some problems.

Now don't get me wrong, what I'm tryin to say is the whole world wasn't rollin' along on greased groves. Now that there was peace and the great W. W. Two was over, the niggers, I mean the colored boys, was actin' up! They was goin' on about Civilian Rights and wantin' decent housin' and good jobs and God knows what else. I feel bad for them though, I really do. I mean they ain't never gonna get no where's marchin'! Seems like all they do nowadays is march. They was even one of 'em got heself elected Senator! But what else did they expect? Next thing ya know they'll be talking about running a negro for president! Imagine that! Might as well run a T.V. game show host and vote for him!

Like my granny Herminie used to say, 'If the hound dog's a'sleepin' the mice will play!'

The experts is sayin' all the time that the educational standard is fallin'. Persunally I don't see no problem with the way folks is readin' and writin'!

Fact of the matter was the magazine trade was getting a lot harder to do business in. Seems like every week there was a new publication popping up on the corner newsstands! Every time we or the Russians shot a rocket into space there was another magazine to cover the story! Seems somebody was willing to write a story about anything, long as it had the word 'astronaut' in it!

The astronaut's home town. The astronaut's family. What kind of breakfast cereal do the astronauts eat? There was always a slew of stories. Especially when one of the rocket ships blew up or crashed into the sea.

Sad truth was that Americans was readin' less and less for factual information and more and more for what ya might call your lower intellect fodder.

There might'a been more and more magazines but there sure was less and less writing. There was ads, pictures, ads, photo layouts, ads, quarter page ads, half page ads and full page ads. All with less and less stories.

This simple fact was not lost on J.J. Hobson who reckoned it didn't add up.

It was then he saw an opportunity to add to his swelling bankroll so he could buy that third yacht he had been eyeing out in the Long Island marina. It was becoming a hassle having to take one of his two yachts to the Gulf of Mexico when needed. Besides, people were beginning to talk, only one boat on each coast.

The truth of the matter was that without a major shot in the arm, and real soon, J.J. had given orders that the magazine be shut down and revamped into a gossip magazine fashioned after the wildly successful *National Enquirer*.

After all, if the *National Enquirer* could make a shit load of cash off of printing a shit load of shit, then shit! Why couldn't J.J.?

There was them business smarts that made America great again!

ʒ

Moping in her chair Kate had heard somewhere that when depressed a hot beverage would do you good and so shuffled around her desk and into the little break room/kitchenette which had become fashionable in the New York City offices nowadays.

Two of the copy boys, Phil Smith and Phillip Jones, were also on break and involved in what for them, was a heated discussion. In reality it only ran about 62 degrees Fahrenheit.

"It's Swinger, like the dancing!" Phillip insisted.

"You're too stupid to be smart! It's Slinger, like the guys what cooks yer hash down at the diners!" Phil corrected.

"How can it be Slinger if he's supposed to be a Jew?"

Kate stood in the doorway that didn't have a door and stared.

"I hate to interrupt this month's meeting of Dyslectics Anonymous but if you're on about the writer, it's Singer, as in Singer sewing machines!"

"I told you it had something to do with buttons!" Phil insisted.

"You said 'zippers'!"

"Same thing!"

"Why were you two Einsteins talking about a man like John Lawrence Singer anyway?"

"*Life Magazine*'s running a story on him this month." Phil pointed to a half open mag on the small kitchen table. Kate glanced over at it as she rummaged through the overhead cabinet for a cup.

"A story? Why have they found him?"

"Didn't know he was lost." Both Phils laughed. She decided to shoot craps and attempt to explain something to them as she fixed herself a cup of tea.

"Less than two years after the war he came home, wrote the book which became very famous and, as you . . . as most informed people know, a few months after it hit the best Seller List Mr. Singer dropped off the grid. Hasn't been seen nor heard from since." She began to fill in the multitude of blanks occupying the free rental space which was their minds.

"I thought he got real famous from that book he wrote? War something. War is something?"

"*War is Bad*." Kate pointlessly corrected as she picked the folded open magazine from the table.

"Shoot, anybody can write about war!" Phil boasted.

"Oh, I suppose you could?!" Kate challenged.

"Hell yes! Look at that Russian fella, Tallboy! He wrote about both sides of war. War and peace!"

"Oh, I suppose you could write a whole book that sells millions of copies?" Philip also challenged.

"Either of you ever *read* a whole book?!" Kate challenged without looking up from the article.

"My point is, it ain't exactly rocket surgery!" Phil said.

Kate shook her head as Eric Burdon lyrics flashed through her head. She sang to herself;

We gotta get outta this place, if it's the last thing we ever do!

Kate recognized the article as a rehash of a story they ran about five years back, the same story they reworked and ran every few years as a space filler, a human interest piece. *How great John Lawrence Singer could have been. Where did he come from? Where was John Singer now? Was he even still alive and how did he die? The Presumed Suicide of John Lawrence Singer.*

"Brain candy! Idiot hacks couldn't write a story if their lives depended on it!" She declared. She tossed the mag back onto the kitchen table and left to return to her desk.

Glancing at the clock which read 10:15, Kate decided it was time for lunch. First she would put a call in to her best friend and former college roommate, Googie Gilda.

"I need lunch! You free?" She queried into the transceiver of the desk phone.

What a coincidence! I need a drink! Lobby in ten?

"Lobby in ten!" Kate agreed and grabbed her jacket and handbag. As she moved towards the elevators the blond temp secretary, in great disarray, whizzed past her balling her eyes out. At the elevator bank she frantically attempted to mash the down button through the wall. The doors opened and the operator asked her what floor.

"OUT OF THIS PLACE!" She yelled between sobs.

Kate shook her head.

Poor temps ought to get fucking hazardous duty pay when they're sent over here! She mused.

Googie's family were well connected in New York City and so not only did she have a good position as an executive secretary working under the head of the credit department, (closely underneath the head of the credit department), of Bank Suisse, but due to the fact she was doing her boss, a trick she learned from her mother, she could come and cum and go as she pleased.

Lunch with Googie, a five foot seven blond haired, blue-eyed vamp in training, was always at a fashionable, trendy, upscale, hip, cool Midtown eatery.

Googie's connections got them a seat by a window with a mere phone call and a half hour later Kate was staring across the table at Googie's beautiful, impeccably made-up face at the latest fashionable, in vogue place down on 19th Street. The very upscale eatery known as Maison de la Mauvaise nourriture.

"Oh you're talking about that famous novelist fella that, that wrote that book and got all them awards after he went away to that war!" Googie proudly brandished.

"Oh you remembered." Kate paid in faux compliment.

"Well I wouldn't know nothing about him."

"Thanks. I knew you were the person to talk to." Their two top table next to the window afforded a panoramic view of the entire six table eatery.

"But I remember Percy mentioned him one time about a week ago." She donated. Kate perked up.

"Really?! Only a week ago?"

"Or was it a month ago? Or might have been a year?"

"You've been with someone for a whole year?"

"No, I guess not."

"Forget it Googie, don't hurt yourself."

"No, no, no, no . . .wait! Percy definitely told me –"

"Who's this Percy guy?"

"A guy. Just a guy. A guy you don't know."

"Which is probably why I asked about him? Come on, give!"

"He's a guy. A banker guy."

"Is it serious? You like him?" Even back in college Kate's altruism manifested itself in the way she looked after her friends.

The immaculately costumed waitress breezed by daftly depositing the dishes in their mini table and kept going. Kate stared down at the two flecks of green next to the bead of red carefully deposited in the center of her big white dinner plate.

"Percy knows stuff about the world. He's educated."

"You went to college!"

"Yeah, but he learned stuff."

As Googie spoke Kate picked up her trendy two tined fork poked at the orange fluid drizzled across half the dish and grimaced.

"Who's Percy?!"

"Okay, okay! Yeah, I like him. Kind'a. He's high up in the Stock Exchange."

"How high up?" Kate pushed. Googie didn't respond. Kate smirked and held her hand four or five inches above the table.

Googie shook her head 'no' and with her thumb pointed up.

Kate raised her hand to a foot high above the table. Googie shook her head and continued pointing up. Kate upped the stakes by holding her hand at face level. Googie again signaled no. Kate's hand rose over her head. Googie shook her head. Kate scrunched up her face, cocked her head to the side and stared. Googie then adjusted her own position to help Kate, until a waitress hurried to the table and chastised her.

"MISS! Please get down off your chair before you fall!" With half the restaurant looking on Googie obliged.

Kate leaned in and whispered across the table.

"How old is this guy?!"

"Older." Googie's friend intensified her stare. "A little older, somewhat older. Okay older."

"How much older?"

"Fifty. . . sixty. –ish. Sixty-seven."

"Sixty-seven?! How the hell does he? I mean can he still even-?!"

"He only pays me to be seen with him!"

"To be 'seen' with him. I smell a gold digger!" She accused.

"You want my help or not?" Googie snapped.

"Okay, okay! Who am I to judge?"

"Thank you! The guy that Percy mentioned was Matt, Matt something."

"Do you recall Matt who?"

"Not really, Percy didn't say but he thought it was something to do with advertising or promotion or something. Matt Mat-something." The waitress appeared with the check.

"I'll get this." Pushing her untouched plate away Kate offered.

"No that's okay." Googie insisted fishing through her knapsack-sized shoulder bag.

"You paid last time!" Kate argued.

"As I remember you paid."

Kate unsnapped her purse and produced her wallet but the argument was abruptly terminated when Googie threw a bill on the table.

"Let's go." Googie directed.

"Holy shit!" Kate looked down at the table and swore. Benjamin Franklin smiled back up at her.

"Googie you put –"

"What? Yeah c'mon, I'm late."

"Get some Percy!" Kate quietly declared. "Score one for the geriatrics ward!" She added as she scurried after her friend. "Hey Googie, this Percy got any friends?"

3

If the Hindu holy men are right and reincarnation is a reality, then surely Matt Matlock was at one time a Mexican Chihuahua.

His beady brown eyes continually darted about while his swivel mounted head rotated like that of a coke addicted owl. His five foot five, spindly frame bounced as he walked and he was never without one hand in his pocket. He was the guy Tom Petty had in mind when he wrote the song *Something Big*.

Matlock was returning from his weekly poker game in the back or the St. Vincent DePaul charity shop on Ninth when he decided on a shortcut to Jimmy's Tavern on Pine Street. Unlike most weeks he had done very good for himself pocketing almost 1200 yards before the game was over.

He was halfway down the alley when suddenly he spotted a six and a half foot, knuckle dragging Neanderthal on a collision course less than ten yards ahead.

He quickly glanced right then left and surmised the alley was too narrow to dash past the big man before being spotted. He turned to run but fell over a garbage can before he could make it two steps in the other direction. This was all the confirmation the Alley Oop-like caveman needed to know he had trapped his latest prey.

The part time body guard-full time torpedo was on him like a crooked vice detective losing at a floating crap game. Rats scattered from the two as they wrestled in the garbage and the big man lifted Matlock by the collar from the trash strewn cobblestones and slammed him hard against the brick wall.

"MATLOCK! Where's Big Louie's money?" Nicki the Knuckle growled.

"I got it, I got it knuckles! Honest ta God!"

"How's come I don't sees it?"

"Let me down and I'll show ya!"

With his feet back on terra firma Matlock carefully righted the knocked over garbage can, slowly reached into his breast pocket and produced a stack of hundreds. He started counting out the money, laying each note in a stack on the lid of the ashcan as he did.

"One hundred. Two hundred. See, I told ya I had it!"

Mat counted in cadence. Knuckles carefully watched Matlock watching Knuckles watching him as he fastidiously and deliberately counted. Suddenly he stopped and looked up at his adversary.

"Knuckles, how many times this make, you chasing me for money I mean? Two, three?"

"Four. Four times. Just keep counting you!"

"Okay, okay! Four times. Four. Four, five." Mat counted out. Arms crossed in determination the big guy nodded in contentment.

"Say, Knuckles, what time is it?"

"What time is it? Fer what?!"

"Yeah, I got'a be somewhere by seven."

"Oh. It's nearly five."

"That late! Thanks. Nearly five! Six, seven eight, nine, ten." He finished counting. "One thousand! See," He declared handing the cash over, "I never welsh on a bet! Tell that to Big Louie when you give him the money! See ya!" Mat made a relieved and expeditious egress.

During the Great Depression Matt Matlock, alias Matt Mathews, alias Mathew Murdock would have been a door-to-door bible salesman. The kind that took the money and never returned with a copy of *The Good Book*.

Wanted in 17 western counties of seven eastern states for a variety of offences, Matt Matlock was known for buying 'properties', that is singers, dancers, writers and then selling them back to agents he's already made a deal with essentially shoe horning himself into the deal. Sometimes he would sign a single artist to several agents.

When one scam started wearing a little thin he'd slither into another one.

Kate skated through the massive marble lobby of the Hobson Building into the brass festooned revolving door and was vomited out onto Broadway where she flagged down a cab.

"Bryant Park and step on it!" She ordered and the Puerto Rican cabbie did just that.

Small of stature Kate always took control when she was goal oriented. Or when there was nobody else around. At that particular moment she was infiltrated with a thought that just might lead to an idea which could, conceivably lead to a lead. Might lead her to a one Mat Matlock.

While mulling things over at her desk that morning Kate remembered a story which ran in one of Hobson's magazines six or seven years ago. It dealt with guys buying war medals hocked by down and out G.I.'s and using them to commit fraud. One of the key players picked up by the cops and locked up for a year was a fellow named Mat. Mat Matlock.

Fifteen minutes later the taxi arrived at its destination, that Neo-classical edifice of some import which dominates the corner of 5thAvenue and 42nd Street in Mid-town Manhattan, The New York Public Library.

She took the granite stairs two at a time and made her way past the two giant Library Lions guarding the main entrance, was swallowed up by a second set of large revolving doors and came out into the grand marble lobby. The elderly guard greeted her with a nod and the librarian at the desk greeted her by name.

Kate made her way to the microfiche room, staked out a chair at one of the twenty foot long oak tables and proceeded to the six foot tall file cabinets which covered the entire east wall. She rummaged through the plastic film containers, organized by date, and pulled a half dozen of them from the long, slender metal drawer.

Back at her work station and after adjusting the side blinders on the television-sized microfiche machine, she inserted the first film roll, turned up the screen's lighting and began to crank through the first of the reels.

*** ʒ ***

So it was like a tenacious spy in a James Bond novel that thirty-two canisters of micro film, six Pepsis and two hours after starting her search Miss Kennedy found the article she was searching for.

It detailed the story of how a one, Mat Matlock, was fingered by the long arm of the law along with a couple of other small time hoods after attempting to perpetrate a scam on an undercover vice cop by selling him bootleg tickets to an Elvis Presley concert.

The five hundred ticket scam wasn't that difficult to crack. The name on the tickets was 'Preslie'.

According to the article, following some jail time Matlock kept a low profile but had surfaced about a year ago suspected of being involved in a phony record scam.

This time the Beetles.

Kate read on and lo and behold there was a location mentioned in the article. More like a neighborhood actually but seein' as how she was a native city slicker Kate knew it to be down in the Bowery close to the Village.

*** ʒ ***

With only the Bowery section of Lower Manhattan mentioned in the article Kate researched at the public Library she was forced to get creative.

With $50 swiped from the newspaper's petty cash fund she had some business cards printed up then, appropriately dressed in her cheapest rich-looking rags, spent the next two afternoons loitering around the dives and gip joints in and around East 1st Street. She reckoned that a two bit grifter like Matlock would know enough to steer clear of any place south of Lombardi's on Spring Street.

Lombardi's, founded in 1905, is undisputedly the first pizza joint opened in the U.S.A. It's also the demarcation point of the Wise Guys who inhabit Little Italy who would have no sense of humor about anybody working scams on their turf, which if any fool had the temerity to attempt to display such audacity he would be rewarded with a one way ticket to the bottom of the East River.

Likewise the Tong mob over in China Town, where any gwai lo snooping around would raise a red flag if seen more than twice in the same area. Unless of course he was there to avail of the chicken Lo Mein at Chin Ho's on Mott Street.

Randomly wandering into a corner joint just off East Houston, the fourth place she tried, Kate slipped into a booth towards the back, ordered a Harvey Wallbanger, opened a notebook and pretended to be working away on writing a book. The place was all but abandoned and the middle aged couple who occupied the middle booth were far to enamored with each other to notice anyone else in the room.

After about ten minutes instinct told her this was the kind'a place a kind'a guy like Matlock would haunt and so she dug in for the long haul.

The guy behind the bar was a tall-ish, dark-ish guy and Kate noticed him as he noticed her and she labeled him handsome-ish. After ten minutes or so, when he nearly wiped the word 'Heineken' off one of the pint glasses while eyeballing the young reporter the thirty something bartender found an excuse to wander over to Kate's booth.

"Hi." He lightly babbled.

By way of a return salutation and without looking up, she thrust her empty glass out to him.

"Harvey Wallbanger, light ice extra Galliano."

He took the glass from her hand.

"'Hi' is a salutary verb used as a form of greeting in most English speaking countries." He sarcastacized. There was no comeback. He sent out another probe. "What are you working on?"

"Work."

"You got an adjective to go with that verb?" He prodded. Kate sighed, sat back and made eye contact.

"How about a possessive pronoun? **My** work. The work which allows me to earn money to pay for my rent. Fraud might have said everybody does everything in order to get laid but Mamet said everybody does everything in order to pay the mortgage. I also do it to buy food and, oh yeah drinks. When I can get one. Harvey Wallbanger, light ice extra Galliano." She resumed pretending to work at her fake work.

As she did so he retired to the back bar and made the drink. As he did a muscular female in a white Tee shirt with close cropped, multi-colored hair and tattoos up and down her arms appeared behind the bar and started wrestling the feeder hoses off two of the kegs.

She noticed the bartender eyeing Kate and quietly laughed.

"What!?" He challenged.

"Fer-get-about-it!"

"Forget about what?"

"She's educated, classy and her parents are probably still married."

"Meaning what exactly?!"

"Meaning she don't hate her father."

"You just got your finger on the pulse of everything don't ya!"

"Bring her the drink. Make your move. A saw buck says she shoots ya down."

"You think she's gonna shoot me down?"

"Wit a Nike missile!" She mumbled around the tooth

pick between her teeth.

"Okay Ann Landers, you're on!" He took up the challenge.

He approached Kate, this time from the side in a lame attempt to see what she was writing but she turned before he accomplished his not so clandestine mission and made eye contact.

"Doing some writing huh?" He pulled back on the stick and attempted to regain altitude before he hit the mountain.

"Your powers of observation are immutable." She quipped.

"Thank you!" He smiled.

A sudden pang of pity permeated her person and she pulled back on the barbs.

"Yes, I'm writing. It's an extended synopsis, kind of like a Readers Digest version of a novel." He appeared to be responding to this new facet of this mysterious woman. "It's known as a treatment in the biz."

"You in the movie business?!"

"Something like that. Producer."

The word 'movie', especially when combined with the words to the effect of: 'I'm here to make a -', has magical, hypnotic powers most remain unaware of until they hear the phrase for themselves. At which point they usually lose all touch with reality, go all gaga and have occasionally been known to pee their pants.

"WOW!" He exclaimed.

"Yeah, wow."

"Hey Tats!" He yelled over to the bar. "You remember that guy used to come in here on and off about five or six months ago?" He inquired as the maid behind the bar continued manhandling full kegs from the back storeroom replacing them with empties. She threw the bar towel over her shoulder and with hands on hips looked up into the ceiling activating her radar for a response.

"Short, lanky guy, looked like a drowned rat even when it wasn't raining?" She clarified.

"Yeah, that's him."

"What about him?"

"Looked like a gangster but let on he was a publisher, an agent or something?"

"What's the difference?" Tat responded.

He turned back to address Kate.

"Anyways, this guy comes in once in a while and says he does something with books or something like that."

"'Something' to do with books? Any chance you remember his name?"

"Yeah, something to do with windows or doors or something."

"Mat?" She threw out.

"Yeah! Yeah that's it Mat . . . Mat -"

"Mat Matlock?" She prompted.

"WOW! You must'a read my mind! How'd you know that?"

"Lucky guess. Plus you gave such good clues."

"He shows up again, you want I should give him a message?"

"Yeah, that'd be great." She rummaged through her clutch and passed him a card which he read aloud.

Becka Moody
Assistant Producer
Warner Brothers Film Studios
New York Office
201-MU5- 0920

"NO SHIT! This on the level Sis?"

"Yeah. Studio sent me out here to sniff around for a novel to turn into a film. L.A.'s the place you go to make it big but, there's no substance out there. All the significant talent, especially writing, comes from the

East coast. Always has."

The seed planted Kate finished her drink and got ready to leave. The bartender mustered his courage.

"Hey any chance I can get your number? I mean your personal number."

She threw some money on the table and while the bartender threw a smirk at the Butch barmaid, Kate scribbled a number on the cocktail napkin from the table.

He watched the door swing closed behind her as she left then danced over to the bar.

"Listen I'd like that twenty bucks in fivers if you got it! I need change to go buy a sandwich later." He bragged. She took the napkin from him and turned back to the wall phone hanging next to the register and dialed.

It rang twice, someone picked up and she held it out for him to hear.

Thank you for call Wong's Mushu Palace, how I help you prease?

Less than 72 hours later Kate had three messages at the newspaper's switchboard.

჻

Amongst the messages the operator gave Kate when she returned to the paper late that afternoon was a note from a one carrying the moniker Mathew Dunston III, Publisher and Agent.

There was no address listed but when she rang the number on the pink message memo Kate wasn't at all surprised to hear the tinkle of glasses and the light buzz of conversation in the background wafting over the line. Sounds which were highly indicative of the answeree being in a pub setting.

She was informed that Mr. Dunston would be happy to meet her at six the following evening.

After receiving Kate's fake card which she gave to the real bartender who passed it on to the fake persona

Matlock had assumed for his latest real dodge, that of a publisher, the real caller was obvious. He was pawning himself off as an agent/publisher with connections on the New York scene.

Matlock had in fact met with a one-time, big time agent years ago, at his trial. The then well-known Broadway literary agent, Jacob Goldstein, alias Jimmy The Jew. Goldstein was the man who handled all the business regarding the novel *War is Bad* for its author, John Lawrence Singer. Goldstein had been called as an expert witness by the prosecution to testify against Matlock and his cohorts after they had been indicted for trying to plagiarize the story.

Kate arrived back at the Houston Street bar thirty minutes late on purpose. She reasoned that if this guy was for real he wouldn't miss the opportunity to nail another mark. Plus making him wait would add to the tension giving her the upper hand.

At six thirty she slipped in to the moderately busy gin mill, made her way to the bar and slipped the dyke barmaid a tenner to tip her off as to which one was her man. Tats the barmaid/barman leaned in close to wipe down the bar and nodded across the floor to the second booth.

Kate nodded back. The tall male bartender's earlier description was dead on.

She spied an emaciated, nervous little guy in a plaid sports coat, wrinkled trousers and battered loafers who was lighting a Lucky Strike with the dying butt of the one he had just finished.

He sat as if in need of a fix, cross legged and hunched over, and Kate imagined herself going to do a drug deal as she approached the booth from behind and to the side.

"You Mr. Dunston?" He jumped when she introduced herself.

"Yeah, yeah. Dat's me. Who's you?"

"I'm Becca, Becca Moody. I work for Warner

140

Brothers pictures."

"Missus Moody! Real nice to meet ya!"

"You needn't bother to stand." She said. He wasn't going to. "Actually it's Miss Moody. I'm not married."

"Oh. Hollywood producer, eh?! Yeah I hoid you wus in town. What's shakin' toots?"

"I understand you have some connections in this town?" Kate signaled to Tats for a drink. "Would you like a beer?"

"Sure, why not?" He fired back. "Connections? I'm plugged in like General Electric, Babe. Anybody what ain't hoid of me can only be tagged irreverent!"

"Irreverent?"

"Yeah, you know, not important. Not worth botherin' wit!"

"I see."

"What can I do ya for? You aft'a a agent or somethin'?" He pushed.

"I'm sort of a junior producer. I'm working on a deal and I don't want to just approach any stranger on the street."

"Yeah, I wouldn't do that neither. Especially since I don't know no strangers."

"I guess that's why you were recommended. If I bring it in on budget, I'm looking at a promotion."

"Ain't that sweet?"

"Yeah." She nodded.

"How much of a budget we talkin' here?"

Tats served Kate's Harvey Wallbanger.

"Well, first things first. Can we get a beer as well please?"

"Sure thing Miss Moody." Matlock was impressed Tats knew her name.

"First thing I need is to find a book, a novel, with a strong story. You know, something people can identify with."

"Like what fer instance? A love story?"

141

"No, the budget they gave me was to drop on a movie script in a genre that's more popular nowadays. A movie script that has to be based on a war story, preferably a novel, you know because of the length. They like em long. You know men, it's all about size."

"A war movie huh?"

"Yes, based on a novel so we don't have to pay a script writer."

"But I thought even with a book you still needed a scriptwriter to-"

"I mean pay them to write an original script! It's more expensive that way." She threw out.

"Oh yeah. I get it."

"Where would I find someone who could point me towards someone who handles a writer with a story like that?"

"Depends, how much of a budget are we talkin' here?" Tats passed by and dropped off the beer.

"Well, it's not much of a budget, but we can maybe do a deal with a B List actor. You know any writers?"

"Not off the top of me head but I might know someone who knows someone. What's in it for me?"

"Well, for reference work the Writer's Guild usually hands it off to the Writer's Reference Department of the Guild who has a meeting once a month and sets the rates, but usually it's around ten, fifteen percent of the production budget."

"Writer's Reference Department huh? Sounds good, but how much of a budget are we talkin'?"

"Oh I'm sure it's nowhere near the ballpark of what someone of your caliber is used to." She cajoled.

"I'll work with it. How much?"

"We got'a keep it under a million and a half." She casually delivered. Mat choked on his beer.

"You okay?"

"Yeah, yeah. It's the beer, not my usual brand. A million and a half you say?"

"Give or take." She dismissively commented.

"I think I can work wit dat." He cleared his throat as he spoke. "How soon you need this book, eh . . . novel?"

"Well, in the next few days."

"Nuthin' like leavin' it to the last minute!"

"What can I tell ya? I got deadlines."

"Kind'a tight ain't it?"

"Well, we could expedite things if I could get a hold of the writer directly."

"I still get my ka-mission right?"

"Oh absolutely! As a matter of fact, you give me my lead and if it pans out, I'll give you the direct line to the WGRD. I know the head guy."

"WGRD?" He questioned.

"Writer's Guild Reference Department! I thought you were in the business?!"

"Oh yeah, yeah. I forgot."

"That sound good to you?"

"Yeah, yeah, Uhh . . . Okay, let me make a few calls and I'll get back to ya. That green?"

"We are green Mr. Dunston." They shook hands to seal the deal.

And so it was through this underhanded conniving with an underhanded grafter that Kate would come to meet with Jacob Goldstein. Alias Jimmy The Jew.

ʒ

Back at Steinkopf's office the inter-office intercom buzzed once before his ultra-efficient secretary, Mrs. Dumbarton, flipped it on.

"Editor-in-Chief's office. Harry Steinkopf Editor. How may I help you?"

"WHERE THE HELL YOU BEEN? WHY'D IT TAKE YOU SO LONG TO ANSWER?" Steinkopf shouted into the line.

Unphased the forty-five year old calmly informed

him. For the third time in the last week.

"Right where I am five days a week from half past eight to six o'clock everyday Mr. Steinkopf, right outside your office. What can I do for you Mr. Steinkopf?"

"WHERE THE HELL IS THAT KENNEDY CHARACTER?"

"Well Mr. Steinkopf it's not my day to watch her. Would you like me to track her down?"

"What do we pay you for?!" He slammed down the receiver.

"Because nobody else will put up with your shit, you sexually frustrated old bastard!" She informed her desk.

ζ

Now few folks knows it but there lurks in the shadows a sector of the business world over which political corruption at the highest levels pales in contrast.

Something organized crime, drug traffickin' and white slavery cannot rival in the depths of its evil. It is rumored that the Great Satan himself, when lost for ideas on how to steal men's souls has taken pages from the people who are the disciples of this vile profession.

I'm talkin' 'bout the Publishers.

Sacrilegious, impious and blasphemous the publisher, a shape shifter able to convince the writer he truly represents the artist while at the same time convinces distributors with big labels that he is the cornerstone of their livelihood.

With opinions as clear as a woman's inner most thoughts and whose sworn word is as bankable as a Fanny Mae mortgage account, The Publisher is rivaled only by The Agent with The Lawyer coming in only a close second.

Now, sworn to secrecy Singer's original agent, Jimmy The Jew, was the only one who could reach Singer and then only when there was a payment to be made. And it had been a while since any currency had changed hands.

Jimmy the Jew's office overlooked Times Square facing south and was located up on the 12th and a half floor well below the giant, white neon Chevrolet sign, directly beneath the Canadian Club Whisky sign just above the Admiral Televisions & Appliances sign all of which flashed in syncopated rhythm. Ergo the extra-large bottle of Bayer aspirin permanently stationed on the upper right hand corner of Jimmy's 1937 office desk.

The 12th and a half floor was in reality the thirteenth floor but . . .well you know. There ain't no 13th floors in Manhattan office buildings

New York City rent control regulations and the fact that his was the only office with a window you could almost see out of were the two factors which had kept Jimmy in the same location for the last thirty-nine years.

From the credit page of Singer's novel and the information Matlock gave her Kate was able to trace the publisher, now defunct, and eventually found Singer's former agent, now semi-defunct with one foot in the grave.

Huffing and puffing onto the 12th and half floor landing Kate fell onto a chair set over in the corner to catch her breath for the next few minutes before tracking down office 1205-17.

The peeling, gold leaf lettering on the glass panel of the half oaken door read;

Jacob Goldstein
Literary Agent

ぇ

GUILD APPROVED

She could hear someone rattling around in the office

but had to knock several times until she eventually received an answer.

"IT'S OPEN!"

She stepped through the door into a time warp. The office was a virtual museum of 1930's artifacts and reliquary. Jacob had apparently fallen on hard times.

The free floor space consisted of just enough square footage to navigate from the front door to the desk and then from the desk to a small, partitioned back space, presumably a toilet, so packed with papers, books and miscellany was the small office. A musty odor permeated the air and the Times Square intersection was only detectable by the din of the traffic and mostly obscured form sight compliments of the soot stained windows.

"Mr. Goldstein?" She called into the forest of books, folders and stacked papers. From behind the desk a snow cropped head popped up to spy the well-dressed, awestruck young lady standing in his doorway. His craggy face instantly contorted in anger.

"I'LL BE OUT BY THE END OF THE MONTH GOD DAMN IT! DON'T YOU PEOPLE READ YOUR FAXS?!"

"Mr. Goldstein, I'm Kate Kennedy, form the *New York Time Magazine*."

His crimson face lit up.

"*The New York Times*! Why didn't you say so! Come in, come in!"

"No sir, the *New York Time Magazine*. The Magazine, not the paper."

"Magazine, smagazine! At this point who cares? Come in, come in."

"I wonder do you remember representing an author named Singer? John Lawrence Singer?"

"Have a seat, have a seat. You want a coffee?" He offered as he fumbled with a vintage aluminum coffee percolator perched on a hot plate that wouldn't switch on.

"Ah, no thank Mr. Goldstein." Kate lifted a large stack of papers from a bent wood chair and sat them on the desk. After she cleared some room on the desk.

"Yeah, I remember him. How the hell could I not?! He was half genius, half artist and half nut job that is until he decided to go off and find a hole to crawl into."

"Any idea where he is?"

"No!" Suspicion was immediately raised at his abrupt answer but she was too much of a professional to push the issue. She filed it away for later.

"Okay, Any idea why he did it?"

"How the hell should I know?! I look like Dear Abby?! I ain't no mind reader!" Kate realized she had struck a nerve.

"Okay, why do you suppose he did it?!" Goldstein relaxed a bit, scanned her up and down then decided she was no immediate threat

"He got drunk one night, with me I mean, and he . . . kind'a opened up. Real unexpected like, but I appreciated it so I listened."

Kate took the hint and lowered her reporter's pad and Bic ball point pen.

"Here's a young guy, wanted to go to medical school, be a doctor, save people, you know the routine."

"Altruistic."

"Exactly, altruistic!" He concurred. "Just back from the greatest war the world has ever seen, saw some heinous crimes against people. All the time he's got'a be thinking, 'Jesus! These are people doing this! People doing this to people!' Rape, torture, death on a biblical scale! 'How can this happen?!' he asks himself. So naturally he starts to doubt everything he's ever been taught."

"Uh huh."

"Then, right near the end of the war, in '45, his company is assigned to take a village inland on

Okinawa. Well, as expected, the Japs are spreadin' propaganda all over the place and one of the things they tell the people is that if the Americans capture them, they will kill the mothers and eat their babies."

Kate nodded as she remembered reading an article on the island hopping campaign in *Life Magazine*.

"So after three continuous days of bloody fighting Johnny and his guys take the village but when they do their last sweep through, they stumble on a group of young mothers and their babies who had been hiding out in the caves. When they send the medics in to check the mothers out and bring them some food, the mothers run screaming towards the cliffs, stand there clutching their kids and jump off the cliffs. Johnny, who's been at the fighting now better than two and half years can't take it anymore. Remember, he's a medic, he's seen the most gruesome wounds men can inflict on one another, but this! This is the last straw. He cracks up. Who wouldn't fer Christ's sake?"

Jimmy pulled open a desk drawer and produced a bottle of Slivovitz and a pair of small glass. "You want?" He offered. Kate nodded and he poured two glasses.

"L'Chyiam!" He raised his glass.

"Slàinte!" She answered and they drank.

"So where'd you leave it?" She asked.

"He got an honorable medical, six months of psychotherapy and was unemployed for most of '46 and '47 til someone suggests he write a book. A book telling it like it really was. Not the John Wayne, Alan Ladd bullshit you see in the movies but the blood, guts and mental damage you actually see in a war."

"Kind of like *All's Quiet on the Western Front*? Hence the popularity of the novel?"

"Not really."

"Not really?!" Kate, having never read the book, assumed it deserved all the accolades it had garnered but sincerely thought she had a handle on the motivation behind its creation. She didn't.

"You ever seen any pictures of Johnny back in the Forties?"

"Only picture I've ever seen of him was the head shot on the dust jacket."

Jimmy reached into the bottom drawer of his desk and pulled out a small folder. He flipped through it and handed Kate a black and white of a guy, early twenties wearing only a Marine issue pair of swim shorts. He stood next to a palm tree on a beach somewhere in the Orient. The guy, tall and muscular sported wavy black hair, and a well sculpted torso and legs. His wall-to-wall smile flashed a set of pearly whites any politician would kill for.

"Jesus! Looks like the guy out of the Charles Atlas body building ads you see in the back of magazines!"

"He was a looker, and that fact was not lost on the ladies!"

"I can see that. So then what happened?!"

"Johnny's on liberty with his shipmates one weekend, somewhere in Hong Kong I think, and he's feeling pretty depressed, see? So one of his buddies spies a good looking dame sitting by herself at a corner table. So, good mate that he is he sashays over there and invites her to join them with the idea of fixing Johnny up, get him out of the doldrums, ya know? She refuses so he buys her a drink anyways, only he tells her the drink is from Johnny! She lays her peepers on Sergeant Singer in his fancy-schmanzy dress uniform and it's all over but the cryin! Now, even with his clothes on, Johnny stills knocks 'em dead."

"Meaning?"

"Meaning that the innocent bar pick-up turned out not to be so innocent."

"Meaning what exactly?"

"Meaning they hit it off and it was, as they say, the beginning of a beautiful friendship. He started his

149

journey back towards normality, writes the book and is turned down by every editor and publisher in the greater New York area. She returns to The States and resumes her senior editor duties at the New York offices of Rank Publishing." He waited for the penny to drop and by the look on her face, it did.

"Rank Publishing! That's who owns my magazine!"

"I know that Sparky! Why the hell ya think I agreed to talk to ya!" Kate's face turned white as she fell back in her chair. "You okay?" Jimmy asked. By way of an answer she held her glass out to Goldstein and he poured her another brandy.

"Are you telling me that Rank Publishing owns the rights to Singer's novel?"

"I don't know if the current status of the contract but Rank Ltd. were the first at it."

"I'd better get over and check on that!"

"Won't do you any good."

"Why not?!"

"Because I distinctly remember a clause in the contract saying he has first right of refusal over any second runs or subsequent re-publications."

"GREAT! Now all I got'a do is go find him!" She gathered her things and tight roped to the door. "Thanks for the drink Mr. Goldstein! It's been an education." As she was halfway out the door he called back to her.

"Hey Kennedy!" Kate turned back to look at Jimmy sheltered behind his ancient desk. "Always remember, every man seeks his own Serenity."

With the trace of a rumor nearly two decades old Kate had her most important lead so far. But didn't yet realize it.

With a plethora of background information but precious little on the current location of John Lawrence Singer, Kate headed back down town to gather her thoughts and set her next strategy.

Struck with a sudden pang of guilt Jimmy, poured

himself another drink, shrugged and quietly mumbled.

"Fuck it! About time he comes out of his shell anyway!" He threw back his drink.

3

Back in the dark confines of Steinkopf's office the tiger waited to pounce.

Kate stepped off the elevator and was spied from across the vast space by Mortimer Needlebaum, the company mail boy as she dropped her coat and bag at her desk. As if he were The Flash incarnate, Mortimer suddenly appeared in front of her desk.

"Oh my God! Oh my God! Oh my God!" He blurted out.

"Mortimer, take a breath! You're hyperventilating!"

"Oh my God Kate!"

"Oh my God Mortimer!"

"He . . . he . . . he-"

"Are you stuttering while trying to laugh or you trying to tell me something?"

"Steinkopf, Steinkopf . . . Steinkopf is –"

"Mortimer, the moon rotates around the earth, the tides go in and out, the sun rises in the east and sets in the west and Steinkopf is probably pissed off at me." She patted him on the shoulder, grabbed her note pad and headed to Steinkopf's office. "It's called the circle of life. It'll be okay Mortimer." She called back as she walked up the aisle.

Initially upset at the fifty dollars missing from the petty cash fund Steinkopf's perpetually simmering wrath boiled over when he discovered no one could actually tell him where Kate had been for the last week.

She knocked and not waiting for the customary grunt came in through the door ready to do battle. Steinkopf sat perched at his desk mutilating somebody's story.

"I know why you called me in here." She reasoned

that she'd fire the first volley, he wouldn't expect that and it might take him off guard.

"SO YOU THOUGHT YOU'D STORM YOUR SKINNY BUTT IN HERE AND FIRE THE FIRST VOLLEY TO TAKE ME OFF GUARD BY TELLING ME YOU KNOW WHY I CALLED YOU IN HERE, HUH?!"

The best laid plans.

"Yes I know why you called me in here."

"OH YOU DO, DO YOU?"

"Yes. You need to know what I've been-"

"Working on?! Yes I would very much like to know what the hell you've been working on for the last week with no proofs, no drafts and no permission from the editor. Ahh, that would be me, thank you very much!"

"I can explain. All I need you to do is-"

"All you need ME TO DO? How about all I need YOU to explain to ME is why YOU took it on yourself to pull fifty bucks from petty cash without clearing it with me first, go gallivanting all over town and then have the unmitigated gall to-"

"HARRY!" She yelled and he nearly jumped out of his seat. He sat upright and glared at her. "Mind if I get a word in edgewise?" She growled at him. "One word, that's all I'm asking. Too much to ask?" He growled back, a little louder.

"Singer." Was all she said.

"Sing her what? What the hell you tryin' to tell me?"

"I think I know where John Lawrence Singer is."

"HUH!" He responded. "Bullshit!" He stared her down. She fell back in her chair.

"Okay, I'm pretty sure I know where I can find John Singer."

"And? So what if you do?"

"So what if I do?! You have any idea what that could mean?! It could save the magazine Harry!"

Steinkopf looked shocked.

"Yeah, I know about Hobson's plans to shut us down and revamp the publication into a supermarket rag. Hell the whole staff knows! Who could be so naïve as to believe a thing like that could be kept a secret?"

"Allow me to reiterate myself. Bull-shit!" He countered.

Pushed to the brink by Steinkopf's bullying she decided to shoot the wad.

Kennedy gripped both arm rests of the chair pushed herself up, marched to the door and held it open. The din of typewriters and ringing phones flooded the office.

"What do you see Harry?"

"What?"

"Tell me what you see!"

"Workers. A room full of people!"

"Wrong Harry. That's a room full of all that stands between tyranny and freedom. All that stands between the facts as they are and the facts as the politicians want us to see them. You know that part on the old *Superman* T.V. show, 'Truth, justice and the American Way?' That's the truth part right out there Harry. The truth part that's supposed to be part of The American Way. But lately it doesn't seem to be that. The American Press seems to have deteriorated into a gaggle of one upmanship on who can boost revenue the highest by spinning stories regardless of the facts or what can be proven or independently corroborated!"

Unimpressed and without comment Harry shifted in his seat.

"That's not a good thing Harry. A room full of journalists. Investigators, the same investigators who are capable of getting to the bottom of any story."

"It doesn't matter and you know why?"

"Why?"

"Because trust me when I tell you no one will ever go broke underestimating the stupidity of the American public, that's why."

"Is that so Steinkopf?"

"Yeah that's so, Kennedy!"

There was a meek knock on the door and the secretary poked her head in.

"NOT NOW!" They yelled in unison and she pulled back out and slammed the door shut. Kate resumed.

"We're in here discussing the future of this publication. Okay let's cut to the chase! I see a day Harry, God help us, when anybody is gonna be able to reach into their pocket, pull out a little handheld gadget , punch in a code and get any kind of information they want! Then people will have stopped reading newspapers altogether and this new . . . electronic media will be controlled by a central source rendering reporters, writers and editors all obsolete and when that day comes John Q. Public will have completely lost faith in all news media! Think that's all bullshit?!" Harry cringed. He didn't approve of women using profanity. Kate leaned forward in her seat and put both arms on his desk.

"Harry, I know that in reality, deep down you're not a son-of-a-bitch, prick bastard, that's just a front. And I also know that you're just as shit scared as the rest of us of Old Man Hobson pulling the plug. But Harry, I've got the torch that can lead us out of the cave Harry! All I'm askin' you to do is let me hold it up! I've got the plug that can stop the leak in the dam! All I'm askin' Harry is for you to let me plug the leak!" She stood up. "Harry let me shove it in the hole so we can all feel good!"

Sweat soaked and exhausted she fell back into her chair, arms draped over the rests. A year and half seemed to pass without response from her boss man.

"Awright Kennedy, you talk a good game. But if you're wrong-"

"I'm not Harry. I know I'm not!"

"If you're on a wild goose chase that fifty bucks, your last week's wages and any expenses are coming out of your pay. Oh yeah, and you're fired!"

"That's what I've always admired about you Harry, your ability to empathize."

"Get the hell outta here!"

Kate left and headed back to her desk.

"No pressure mind you!" She told herself.

ȝ

Always remember, every man seeks his own –

Kate had been mulling over Jimmy the Jew's words. Stretched out on the couch in the kitchenette of the office, she laid there for the last hour and a half repeating the mantra Jimmy the Jew had left her with two days ago.

Every man seeks his own Serenity. "Why would he say that? So totally out of context?"

Remember, every man seeks his own Serenity.

"SHIT!" Kate finally hit on the idea of resorting to harsher measures.

Springing from the couch she dashed to the elevators and took the first car down to the basement where the corporate research library was located.

The corporate researcher was an important office in every large corporation and as an indication of their status in the company, they were always located in the basement.

Normally staffed by two to three ladies they were headed up by a certified librarian who catalogued and was thoroughly familiar with the plethora of various reference volumes, texts and catalogues the company library contained. It was a library dedicated to referencing for the company and its executives.

It was nearly five o'clock and Beatrice, the 42 year old, unmarried librarian, the last one left in the reference room, was about to lock up.

Beatrice! Thank God I caught you!" Kate shoehorned

155

herself through the door and into the large room which resembled a mini-offspring of the New York Public Library.

"Kate, it's five to five, it's quitting time! Can't this wait till tomorrow?!"

"Beatrice, this is very, very important. It has to do with possibly giving Hobson an alternative to shutting us down!"

Beatrice ripped off her coat and threw her handbag on the desk.

"Okay, what do you need?" She grabbed a pen and pad from a drawer and wrote as Kate spoke.

"I need all references you can give me to the word serenity."

"You mean the emotion?"

"Yes. I think. To start, yes. But I'm sure there's more to it."

"Like what for instance? Give something to go on."

"Okay, okay. There's more."

"Like what?"

"I don't know!" Beatrice sighed and sat back in her roller chair.

"Well as long as you've got such a clear idea of what you want, this shouldn't take long!"

"If you start there I'm sure we'll find something."

"Ya know if a frog had wings –"

"I know, I know, he wouldn't bump his as so much! I'm sorry. Let's just start there okay? The word serenity."

Beatrice got up and moved to the Webster's Unabridged Dictionary sitting opened on the large oak book podium at the end of one of the book aisles.

"From the Latin serinitas; to mean clear or fair. Applicable as an adjective or, in the case of a title of royalty, as a noun." She turned to Kate. "You been making nice-nice with a king or kiss any frogs that turned into a prince lately?"

156

"Lots of frogs yes, princes not so much!"

"Well, there's always locations." She moved to an atlas reference encyclopedia and flipped through it. "I have a Serenity Bay. That's in Florida. Serenity Airport in Arizona. Serenity Cove in Goose Bay and a Serenity Township in North Eastern New Hampshire." She turned to get Kate's response but was answered only by the swinging of the door on its hinges. "YOU'RE WELCOME!" Beatrice yelled after Kate.

Ƹ

Wrestling the steering wheel of the rented two-tone, Chevy Impala, convertible Kate attempted to keep one eye on the road, one eye on the wildly flapping county map and one eye on the exit signs which came with increasing frequency.

Serenity, New Hampshire
Next Right

She barely made the turn-off.

As she took the first left she was greeted with a 3D, pop-up post card of a scene from *Holiday Inn* with Bing Crosby.

Colonial wooden, clap board homes tastefully painted in light pastel shades with white trim lined both sides of the four lane street. The black top road lead tastefully to a Presbyterian church at the end of the main street topped with a cross crowned cupola tastefully surrounded with a widow's peak.

All of course tastefully painted in white.

In the Spring and Summer, she imagined, there were plush maple trees for shade and in the Winter layers of tufted soft snow for skiing and frozen ponds somewhere for ice skating.

A large square sign with scalloped edges greeted each

visitor.

No alcoholic beverages

No littering

No cigar smoking or spitting on the sidewalk.

No cycling or nude hoola hooping in public.

No loud noises after 10 p.m.

Welcome to Serenity! The sign was painted white.

Serenity was New Hampshire's oldest settlement, dating back to 1619, one year before the pilgrims landed at Plymouth Rock. At least that was the claim.

Of course the history books, government and town hall records still showed that it was founded in 1710 A.D. But desperate times called for desperate measures.

It was no coincidence that the revised date of *Serenity's* founding began to appear on all the signage lining the tourist routes, on the tourist brochures and all the travel manuals in all the book shops across New England only ten years ago. It was ten years ago, in an emergency meeting of the Town Fathers, that it was decided something was needed to boost tourist attention. Ten years ago exactly that a massive outbreak of dysentery seized all of Wyatt County.

The desperate times began with the great water scare back in September of '51 when the Bergen County Water Treatment facility spilled its entire sewage tank into the fresh water reservoir supply line which was so serious that it garnered a thirty second spot on the ABC Six O'clock News.

The intensive investigation which followed, costing the town $12,576.47, revealed that Reggie Faultmeyer forgot to replace the lynch pin to the dump tank in the sewage room before he clocked out one night.

Of course Serenity still had bragging rights to the World's Largest Cast Iron Skillet just off the road on Maggie Maybelle's farm just off Route 2. But it wasn't drawing the crowds it used to ever since they put in the interstate. Plus the people from Guinness still hadn't flown over from Ireland to verify that it was actually the largest skillet in the world, but nobody challenged Maggie's claim.

If you looked in Webster's under the word 'normal', there would likely be a picture of Serenity, New Hampshire, population 14,207, established in 1710 A.D. Or 1619.

Nothing strange or out of the ordinary ever happened in Serenity. Nothing except the occasional strange happenings out on Route 2a, Box 32 at the foot of Spencer's Mountain.

Kate drifted slowly through all three blocks of the town center and pulled a U-turn at the top of Main Street in front of the All Souls United Presbyterian Church.

She then turned off the main street and circled back just as a police siren sounded and a red light began flashing in her rear view mirror.

"SHIT! Welcome to Serenity." She mumbled.

She pulled over and, through the side mirror, watched the short, chubby cop struggle out of the town's single patrol car and waltz up to the driver's side of her car, ticket book in hand.

"You ain't from aron hair, are ya?"

"Excuse me?"

"I say, you ain't from aron hair, are ya?"

"Ahh, no I'm not officer."

"U-turnin's a-legal hair!" He declared. Kate had to think fast.

"Sorry officer but, I had to turn around to see the sign again. I can't see a thing without my glasses."

"Oh. Well okay but I still gotta give ya a ticket young lady. I mean what'd happen ta this town if we just let anybody go hot rodin' up and down the streets at all hours'a the day and night?!" Licking the tip of his pencil he began writing away. Kate kicked it in to second gear.

"I could see . . . sniff . . . I could see how that would become . . . sniff . . . a problem officer." She reached for

159

a tissue from the glove box.

"What's the reason for ya visit here in Serenity?"

"I'm here to find . . . sniff . . . to see my long lost father. We haven't seen each other since I was a little girl. His name is John Lawrence Singer." She peeked one eye on the cop to gauge for a reaction. Nothing.

"That's a wicked good reason miss – " He perused her license and squinted down at her.

"If your father's name is John Singer then how come your license says Kennedy? You ain't tryin' ta pull one over on me are now?"

"Oh God no officer! You see, my mother was so broken up by the divorce – sniff, she . . . she changed the children's name when he left."

"Your parents is da-vaced? So's mine! Well, technically. They shot each other durin' an argument. They was both on the force. Terrible thing, da-vorce!" He stopped writing.

"Isn't it though? My parents separated after he was diagnosed with sickle anemia."

"OH my god! That's devastatin'!"

"Yes I can only pray he's still alive."

"Wait a minute! I thought only black folks get that disease?!"

"That's what took us all by shock officer! The first white man ever to contract what was previously believed to be only a black disease! Experts came from miles around to examine him. Pretty soon he got sick of all the attention and just, just . . .sniff . . . disappeared." The cop lowered the book and pencil. "Without a trace." She added. "Sniff!"

"Sounds like a case of missin' persons to me."

"Actually, you being connected and all, I mean access to the FBI, The CIA, the Elks Club, you might be able to help me find him. I have reason to believe he's right here in Serenity. Someplace."

"Well, I ain't got no ability to call the CIA or the

FBI, and I can only invoke the powers of the Elks Club on the first Thursday of the month, that's when we meet up, but you might try John Proctor's place. That'd be the general store. Just down the street."

"OH MY GOD OFFICER, officer - ?"

"Hathorne, officer Judge Hathorne. The Third."

"What an interesting name, officer Hathorne!" She took his hand and made direct eye contact. "Now I realize, for the first time, why New Englanders are constantly voted the Warmest People In a Cold Climate Environment by the American Humane Society of Humanists every year! Thank you, thank you, thank you!" He blushed. She drove off without a ticket.

Two blocks away she parked the car around the corner and made her way into John Proctor's Feed, Groceries & General Store.

The double front door opened into the side of an unusually long, rectangular floor plan with the check-out counter and register to the left by the door.

She counted four full aisles running the length of the store with a loft over the back third. There was a staircase leading to the basement to her right and all manner of any item man, woman or child might desire to purchase plastering all available wall space or hanging from the ceiling.

"Howdy Ma'am. What can I do ya for?" The well-worn wooden boards creaked under her feet as she pretended to peruse some items in the first aisle. She turned to the old man in the spotless white, bib apron behind the counter and as she drew closer she noticed that the lines in his face had lines in them.

"Well, sir-"

"Call me John!"

"Okay John, I'm Kate, and I'm looking for a . . . supposing I was looking for a place where I could get away from it all? An isolated place where . . . a place where I could just concentrate on my writing. Maybe take a walk every once in a while, but not too far out. Still in proximity to the town where I could buy groceries and other necessities when I needed to." As she spoke an old woman, also draped in an apron and roughly the age of the man, appeared up from the basement staircase. "Where would I find such a place? Around here I mean." Kate finished. The old woman slowly ambled over to the counter.

"This is my sister, Mary." The man introduced.

"Pleased to meet you Mary." Both were easily octogenarians.

"Likewise." She grunted.

"Would you know of any such place John?" The reporter probed. The sibling exchanged glances.

"Ah . . ." John stuttered. Mary cut him off with a mighty yell up at the piñata packed ceiling.

"MA! MA COME OUT HERE!" The sound of tumbling items emanated from somewhere in the back and shuffling could be heard. A few minutes later, with the speed of molasses rolling uphill in winter time, an ancient woman slowly emerged from behind the counter display of chocolates and breath mints to Kate's right.

"MA, TAKE THIS LADY IN THE BACK AND HELP HER OUT." Mary pointed to her ear to indicate the reason she was yelling. Apparently Ma was hard of hearing.

"This here is our ma. Ma Tituba. Follow her to the back and she'll help ya out.

Kate was uneasy at the strange request but followed along.

Tucked way back in the far corner of John Proctor's General Store was a small, barred window which had been carved out of the wall. Just above the window a sign read:

General Post Office

Kate arrived at the window several minutes before the atavistic woman and so waited impatiently as she shuffled to the back. There was a slight commotion behind the window and a moment later the shade was pulled up and, like a teller at a bank, the prehistoric woman materialized behind the bars.

"How can I help you young lady?"

"WELL, I'M LOOKING FOR-"

"Why in tarnation you yelling? You deef or something?"

"No, no! Your daughter said you were-"

"Hard of hearing?! Well I ain't. Hear as good as you, probably better! I just likes messing with them two BB stackers. Besides I can hear 'em when they talk about getting rid of me so they can enjoy their youth."

"YOUTH?! They're at least . . . never mind. As I was asking your children – "

"Children? HA! Punishments more like! Two ain't got a brain between 'em! Dummer than a box'a rocks!"

"Ah . . .okay."

"You say you're looking for a place near here?"

"Yes, yes but, do you mind if I ask you . . . your name is Tituba?"

"What about it?"

"And your children are Mary and John?"

"What about it?"

"Arthur Miller?"

"Never heard of him. He English?"

"Just out of curiosity, the church at the end of the road?"

"All Souls United Presbyterian Church, yeah, what about it?"

"The preacher's name wouldn't happen to be Reverend Parris? Is it?"

"Oh, you know him?"

"No, nothing. Never Mind."

"Look here get to the point. I got a crap game I got'a

hurry up and get to. Starts in a couple'a hours."

"Where?"

"Across the street. Now what'a ya want?"

"I'm looking for a place where I can get away from it all. An isolated place where I could just concentrate on my writing. Maybe take a walk every once in a while, but not too far out. Still in proximity to the town where I could buy groceries and other necessities when I needed to. Where would I find such a place? Around here I mean."

"Bullshit!"

"What?!" Kate feigned shock. The antediluvian woman passed her a tissue through the bars.

"What's this for?"

"You're so full of shit it's coming out yer ears! I'll be a hundred and seven next September and you think this is my first rodeo!"

"What do you mean?"

"Every year or so some fortune seeker meanders up around these parts with some cock and bull story looking for that missing writer fella." Kate didn't reply. "You ain't really looking for a place to settle down and write are ya? Probably some ego-inflated reporter who thinks they got a book in 'em, prob'ly a novel or somethin'!" Ma Proctor pushed. Kate responded by leaning in and lowering her voice a decibel or two.

"Girl to girl, no I'm not. Truth of the matter is I'm looking to locate my long lost father. He contracted a terrible disease some years back and shortly after being diagnosed he thought it best to divorce my mother and –"

"Spare me! That the best you got? You're supposed to be a reporter. How in the hell you gonna get to the bottom of a story with a lame cover like that?"

Kate, taken off guard, sighed deeply and composed herself.

"Look Ma, cut me some slack will ya?! I been on this

case trying to find this guy for last week and half and all I keep coming up with is bubkis!"

"Zero, huh?" Ma backed.

"Yeah, Zilch."

"Snake eyes!"

"Danada."

"Nichts."

"Nienta!"

"So what ya trying to say is, ya got nothing?"

"Bottom line is, if I don't come up with something and soon, I'm on the street!"

"Ya know young lady, we ain't supposed to say nuthin' on account'a all the money he gives to the town council for upkeep and what not. He gave a pie-anna to the school last year. Nice one too!"

Kate slid a twenty underneath the bars of the window. Tituba quickly snatched it away.

"Ya know I'll catch hell if the town's folk ever find out I spilled the beans."

A second twenty found its way underneath the bars and across the narrow counter. It joined its mate in Tituba's side pocket.

"Route 2a, Box 32. Can't miss it. It's just at the foot of Spencer's Mountain. South of town."

"Ma, I owe you my life!"

As Kate left Ma called dafter her.

"You got a gun, Honey?"

"No, why?"

"He can be a cantankerous bastard given a reason."

ჳ

The long, winding road which led uphill for a quarter mile terminated at a lone house perched on the top of a smaller hill and was set back from the road by a couple of hundred yards.

The big Chevy slowed as it approached the split level

bungalow which fit the description the young gas station attendant gave her when she stopped for directions fifteen minutes ago.

There was someone on his knees, working back near the house. As the car drew closer she could see, with his back towards the road, the older man tinkering in the plush front garden. The man glanced up as the car pulled alongside the hydrangea bushes bordering the front of the property.

"God damned hippies! No respect!" He cursed as if the visitor wasn't two hundred yards away.

He pushed up from where he was and hobbled towards the road. Kate stepped out of the car to greet him. He hesitated, did an about face and hobbled back into the house re-emerging with a double barreled, side by side shotgun fumbling with the cartridges as he tried to load the weapon.

"God damned hippies! I'LL GIVE YOU TILL THE COUNT OF THREE TO GET OFF'A MY PROPERTY! Psycho female!"

"OR?" She challenged but retreated back behind the car when she spotted the gun.

"Or I'll shoot your sorry ass!"

"You can't just shoot people who you don't want to talk to!"

"I can't?"

"NO! This isn't the Soviet Union!"

"Okay then, I'll shoot ya then call the cops! This ain't California either, God damn it!"

"Good idea John, shoot me, call the cops then everybody will know where you are." He was momentarily stunned that she called him by name.

"You think I'm joking lady? One . . . two -" He continued to fumble dropping one of the shells which rolled off the path and into the flower bed.

"God damn it!" Kate scurried over, retrieved the cartridge and handed it to him.

"Thank you."

"You're welcome."

He stuffed it into the breach, closed it over and pointed the gun at Kate. She stood fast.

"You know what will happen if you shoot me?"

"You talkin' about the cops? I ain't afraid of no cops!"

"Not cops, worse! T.V. news stations! I can see it all now. Mobs of fans and fanatics outside your house. Gangs of reporters. TALK SHOWS! Let's don't forget the talk shows! The convoys of TV vans! Plenty of room out on that road for oh, half a dozen news vans no problem. What-a-ya think, you're a fan of daytime television, aren't you?"

"Two . . .!"

"You know they're teaching your novel in early Twentieth Century Literature courses now!" He stared at her. "Yeah, they are. They're comparing it to Hemingway, Steinbeck, Nobokov!"

In her research Kate had read of an incident where, in a phone interview, the reporter mentioned Nobokov and his work. Singer became so incensed that he terminated the interview and had his phone disconnected.

"NOBOKOV!? THE *LOLITA* NOBOKOV!? YOU GOTTA BE SHITTIN' ME! *LOLITA*!?"

He moved closer as he ranted. She gently brushed the shotgun muzzle away and stepped to the side. "ABOUT A GOD DAMNED PEDIFLILE? A PERVERTED PROTAGONIST AND A LYING NARRATOR, WHAT THE HELL IS THAT ABOUT? WHERE'S THE EMPATHY?!"

Having hit a soft spot Kate carpied the diem by egging him on.

"A lot of people think it's about true love." She shrugged.

"TRUE LOVE? DID YOU EVEN READ THAT PIECE OF-? HELL NOT EVEN NOBOKOV KNEW

167

WHAT IT WAS ABOUT! HE WAS JUST FISHING FOR PRESS THAT'S ALL!"

"Well, most people do agree that many new writers opt for shock value over substance."

"Hell, that don't make it right does it?! Don't matter who you are or what you do ya still got'a have standards!"

"Yes, but it's always much easier to get attention, get yourself noticed by doing something worse, more shocking, more abysmal then anyone has done it before rather than break new ground. That's too much extra effort." He slowly lowered the shot gun a she spoke.

"Young people agree with that?" He nearly pleaded.

"Oh God no! Not the educated ones." She stepped around behind him. "I mean, nowadays erect nipples under a flimsy dress or wet tee shirt is provocative, it's only a matter of time before we start seeing breasts in movies."

"I don't object so much to breasts. If it makes a statement of course."

"Of course! It's just the shameful exploitation of the visual medium to demean or belittle the artist's original statement that's wrong."

"EXACTLY!" He took a few steps further from the hydrangea force field and it was in confused assessment that he stared at her for a long while.

"Who are you anyway?" He finally asked.

"I'm Kate. Kate Kennedy."

"You are reporter?"

"Not really. I help find missing persons."

"Well you found me now you can go." He brushed past her heading back towards the house.

"You talk to me, off the record if you want, or I have a news van here inside a half an hour." He froze in the door.

"You blackmailing me? On my own property?!"

Kate took several steps back towards the blacktop to

stand in front of the car.

"Not on your property. I'm on the road and that's a public right of way."

"So because you're a reporter you don't need to respect a man's privacy, that it?"

"I said off the record if you want. I promise you unless you agree nothing we talk about will go to print. Besides I'm not blackmailing you. Just offering a deal, that's all."

"Oh a deal huh.? Like voting for the worst of two candidates, eh?"

"As if you've never done that before?"

"Alright, I'll give you that."

"Five minutes, that's all I'm asking for."

Without rejoinder he retreated to the house and emerged a few minutes later with two aluminum folding chairs a bottle of 12 year old Glenlivet and two glasses. He was also minus the shot gun.

"All I really need to-" She started.

"SHHHH!" He shushed her and set up the chairs under the pear tree in the garden. Kate took a seat as indicated and perused the plush, slightly overgrown garden as he poured two drinks. Singer produced a tree stump which he set between the chairs and employed as a table for the drinks and the bottle before he stretched out on the other chair, folded his legs at the ankles, leaned back and closed his eyes.

"Mr. Singer, I really only-"

"SSSHHHH, SSSHHHHH!" He passed her a drink and sipped his own. He pointed to his position which Kate slowly emulated.

After only a minute or two her senses focused on the light breeze rustling the through the branches, the mixed aromas of the flowers and the gentle chirping of the unseen wrens in the hydrangeas. She felt a calmness blanket her psyche. After a full five minutes he spoke.

"Get it?" He whispered and although she told her

mouth to respond her brain told her to wait. It took her a long moment to answer.

"Yeah, yeah I do."

"Good. Now we talk."

"I'm relieved to finally have a chance to get it all off my chest." He spoke softly, barley above a whisper with his head back and eyes closed.

"All what?"

"This whole scam thing."

"What scam?" Kate probed.

"The phoniness of the whole thing."

"I'm sorry Mr. Singer, I'm not following you."

"It's John. The book. My book. *'The greatest piece of post war literature to hit the stands'*!" He mocked. "It was a piece of shit! I was drunk half the time I was writing it!"

"But it was a hit, a huge hit!"

"Never underestimate the stupidity of the American public dear girl. The overwhelming majority of people in this country still believe in angels, gods, flying saucers and the Devil! Hell, NASA's fixing to send a man to the moon in the next ten years and they'll no doubt be buffoons who'll say it's all a conspiracy!"

"But why did you quit the whole scene? You could have had a film contract, lived on Easy Street and kept on writing!"

"I did."

"Did what?"

"I did get offered a film contract. A couple of them as a matter of fact."

"Jesus what happened?!"

"I told them to shove it!" He sipped his drink.

"In God's name, why man?!"

"Art? Talent? It's all bullshit. Art and talent don't mean a damn thing in the publishing industry today! Never even figure into it. It's all about how much money can we make off of this book? Doesn't matter how big a piece of shit it is all that's important is the question; 'Can we spin it into a golden egg?'"

"Meaning a best seller?"

"Meaning a best seller which guarantees a movie contract!"

"I apologize if I'm a little slow but-"

"My book was a piece of shit! *War is Bad*?! You call that a title?! It's embarrassing! I'm ashamed my name's on the cover."

"That wasn't your original title?"

"Are you serious? How thick do you think I am?! My working titles were *Death of a Soul. Morality Fades. Hell in the Pacific. The Demise of Morality.*"

"I see." Kate hadn't been that heavily disillusioned since Raymond Chandler died a couple of years ago. She sipped her drink. Singer continued.

"It's nothing to do with talent! Why do you think best sellers almost never win any significant prizes?"

"Like what?"

"Like a Noble or a Pulitzer? They're all well spun mind candy that's why. No statements, nothing to say, nothing to inform the general public of – "

"Of the true horrors of war for instance?"

"Exactly!"

"Are you saying people don't want writing of substance?"

"Riddle me this Batman; Why are all the Noble Prize and Pulitzer books not bestsellers? At least not until they've won the award?"

"I did not know that!" Kate was stunned.

"Answer's easy. The idiot people need somebody to tell them what's good. What they should read, what they should see at the movie house." He poured two more drinks. "Don't get me wrong, there has to be a certain amount of talent. At the very least you have to learn the mechanics of the trade. True for any trade. But the main thing is - the whole thing is dictated by what they can sell. Doesn't matter how good or bad it is. How many works become classics years after the authors are dead and gone?"

Kate began to see his argument. He pressed his point further.

"Ever ask yourself; 'How did such a shitty movie get made?!' Well chances are it was made from a shitty book! How'd that book get published? Some publisher connived to get a movie made so that he could manipulate it from a book contract. Somebody knew somebody who had a friend who had a friend."

"Okay so it's on the publishers, but they can't all be bad!"

"Lemme tell you something Sweetheart, you could take all the sincerity in the publishing industry, stuff it in the naval of a firefly and still have room for 3 or 4 caraway seeds plus the heart of a publisher."

"Too late to get it sugar coated?"

"That was sugar coated! Most publishers are failed writers. Then again, so are most writers. Most wouldn't know talent if they tripped over it!"

"Jimmy the Jew thought you had talent." She offered.

"Jimmy the Jew?! If he had cannibals for clients he'd promise them missionaries for dinner. Of course he'd say I had talent, he took me on didn't he? I was a steady meal ticket for as long as the ride would last."

"He hinted you guys had a pretty good relationship."

Singer sat back and lightly nodded.

"Yeah, we got on alright I guess. I wrote it, he sold it. It was like the love scene in a James Cagney movie. You know, the one where he lets the other guy live. He was on the down and out, on his way down to the skids. He knew I was a schmuck, and that I'd sign with the first guy that waved a contract in front of my face."

"So you never wrote again? I don't get that."

172

Singer stared at her, a creepy look like the look you'd imagine a mass murderer had painted on his face right before he set out to do his dirty deed.

Finally he spoke.

"Wait here. I got something for you." Singer once again disappeared into the house. Kate glanced at her wrist watch. Three quarters of an hour had passed.

He returned with a sheaf of papers wrapped in plain brown paper. The package had a sealed envelope Scotch taped on top of it.

"Don't open this until you're back in New York. Deal?"

"You have my word Mr. Singer."

"John."

"Can I contact you here?"

"No. Use the post office in Serenity. I have a drop box there. They'll see I get anything you send."

"Again, you have my word, anything I want to publish I'll run it by you first."

Kate turned to leave and was several steps towards the hydrangea ramparts when he called after her.

"Were you serious about that Nobokov crack?"

"No. I was just annoyed because you didn't stick around to fight the rising tide of shit writing ebbing into circulation. Don't you get it John? We need people like you to stick around as long as possible."

Singer smiled and bowed at the compliment.

"I guess you could call *Lolita* a novel of erotic motifs." Singer conceded.

ᢃ

She arrived home that Friday evening and, motivated by her talk with Singer, Kate decided to buy a copy of *War is Bad* at the book shop around the

173

corner from her apartment building. She sat up all night in her one room walk-up and into early Saturday morning reading it. When she finished it that morning she tossed it onto the coffee table.

"Wow! That book was a piece of shit."

Late that afternoon, after meeting some friends for brunch she returned to the apartment, poured a glass of wine and finally decided to tear into the package Singer gave her.

She opened the envelope first and was shocked at the contents. Almost as shocked as she was by the package it was attached to.

3

Late for the Monday morning staff meeting which ended an hour ago, Kate scurried from the elevator on the 47th floor. She didn't stop at her desk but went straight for Steinkopf's office. A new temp sat quietly crying at the desk outside Steinkopf's office, this one a pudgy red head.

"I . . . wouldn't go . . . go in there if I were . . . you!" The young secretary sniffled as she dabbed her eye with a soggy Kleenex

"That's why you're you and I'm not." Kate quipped as she breezed by the desk and pushed through the door. Old Stonehead looked up from his desk and sat back in his high back swivel chair. An evil smirk hung from his face.

"Well, well, well, look who decided to show up for work, Dorothy Parker herself!" Kate didn't reply but hung her overcoat on Steinkopf's King Edward coat rack by the door then moved to his desk.

"Brought you a souvenir." He ignored the Macy's shopping bag she plopped on his desk.

"Why are you here?" He challenged before reaching into the bag and retrieving a thick, black seat cushion.

She took it from his hand and carefully placed the thing on the chair in front of Steinkopf's desk before plopping herself into the hot seat and leisurely reclining back.

"Kennedy, I don't know what the hell you're tryin' to pull but your lame excuses of 'real journalism' ain't gonna bail you this time! You're history sister! Yesterday's news, a foot note in the archives! Pack up your desk and sign out with HR!"

"Harry shut up and read what's in the bag."

He pulled the package out and sniffed it.

"What the hell is it?"

"Jesus Harry! What are you a five year old at Christmas?! Open it fer cryin' out loud!"

He dropped the bound manuscript in front of himself and used his scissors to cut the brown twine which held it together.

"*Death of a Soul*!" Harry read aloud from the cover page of what was obviously a manuscript.

"*Death of a Soul* Harry that's what it is."

"Whose soul? Yours because you're all washed up in journalism?"

"To surrender my seat on the express train to diminished expectations all I had to do was excavate the right story Harry. That's what I did."

"Big deal, am I supposed to be impressed?! You keep following up enough leads and that million-in-one long shots usually crops up nine times out of ten."

She reached over and presented him with the white envelope.

"I don't get it. There's no name on this manuscript."

"Have a gander at that." She instructed. Steinkopf read the letter.

Inside the envelope Singer had taped to the manuscript was a certified letter with permission to release the enclosed manuscript under a pseudonym in episodic formats once a week for the first three chapters and then to release the published manuscript one week later.

Harry read the name at the bottom of the letter. John Lawrence Singer.

"This on the level?"

"What'a you think Harry? I believe the words you're looking for are; Thank you Miss Kennedy, I always knew you would ride in here one day on a white horse and save my magazine and all those folks jobs, including mine, because you are the consummate professional I saw in you when I first hired you ergo I am forever in your debt and it would be a pleasure for me to allow you to move into that corner office you so richly deserve. Or words to that effect."

"Now what do you really want me to say?"

"The date and amount of my pay raise."

"What's the catch?"

"Magazine gets the serial rights and any follow-up stories. All royalties of the novel to go to a friend minus expenses and production costs of course."

"Now why in hell would he do that? If this thing is any good we're talking five maybe six figures here!"

"I wondered the same thing so I had the front desk put in a long distance call to New Hampshire this morning before I came up here." Harry growled at the words 'long distance'. "Take it out of my wages!" She snapped. "He wants the money to go to a Marine buddy's wife and kids he served with in Okinawa. The government screwed up the paper work and she never got a dime in death payments. Holding down two jobs to support four kids, one of them disabled."

"Jesus! Raw deal eh? But what about him, he doesn't want anything?"

"Not gonna need it. Turns out he's been diagnosed with terminal lung cancer. A result of the fumes from the gas they bombed the beach with before the Marines went in. Doctors give him six to eight weeks to live."

"Jesus!" Harry fell back in his high backed swivel

chair. "Raw deal!"

ʒ

Well, there you have it folks! And as if that ain't enough, it was J.J. Hobson heself who was persuaded to finance the publishing and ad campaign of *Death of a Soul* by Sue D, Nym, a up and coming young writer to the New York literary scene.

As a matter of fact, the ad and promo campaign was so successful that wasn't nobody, least ways not even Kate herself that suspected the super aggressive campaign J.J. launched would result, a short eighteen months later, in Kate Kennedy, alias Sue D, Nym, stepping out of a limo at the movie premier of the script she wrote herself based on the best-selling novel. But only after the book was nominated for a Pulitzer Prize.

And I almost forgot to tell ya'll, she was accompanied by a tall-ish, dark-ish bartender from down on Houston Street.

ʒ

As Kate sat in Steinkopf's office that Monday morning, Mat Matlock stood, freezing his gonads off, out on the abandoned 12nd Street pier, in Lower Manhattan hopping from one foot to the other attempting to keep warm.

A week later, after they met, as one last bit of business Kate rang the bar down on Houston Street and asked Tats to pass a phone number to Mat Matlock next time he was in. It was a number, Kate said, to the Writers' Guild, Reference Department. The fact was Matlock had been in every day since they met that Friday.

Tats did as requested and when Mat asked to use the bar phone Tats dialed for him and passed him the receiver.

"Yeah, hi this is Mr. Dunston. I was told to call youse about-"

Thank you for call Wong's Mushu Palace. How I help you prease?

ξ

THE END

Also by Paddy Kelly

Ghost Story
(A play)

Operation Underworld

The American Way

Don't Eat To Live, Live To Eat

The Wolves of Calabria

Children of the Nuclear Gods

There's An App For That!

There's An App For That, Too!

Politically Erect

American Rhetoric

Broad in the Kimono

Synopsis or option information available on line at:
www.paddykellywriter.com or by contacting
paddy.incanto@gmail.com